Christina Georgina Rossetti

Verses

Christina Georgina Rossetti

Verses

ISBN/EAN: 9783742814371

Manufactured in Europe, USA, Canada, Australia, Japa

Cover: Foto ©Andreas Hilbeck / pixelio.de

Manufactured and distributed by brebook publishing software
(www.brebook.com)

Christina Georgina Rossetti

Verses

VERSES

BY

CHRISTINA G. ROSSETTI.

Reprinted from " Called to be Saints," " Time Flies,"
" The Face of the Deep."

PUBLISHED UNDER THE DIRECTION OF THE TRACT COMMITTEE.

Fourth Thousand.

LONDON:
SOCIETY FOR PROMOTING CHRISTIAN KNOWLEDGE,
NORTHUMBERLAND AVENUE, W.C.; 43, QUEEN VICTORIA STREET, E.C.
BRIGHTON: 135, NORTH STREET.
NEW YORK: E. & J. B. YOUNG & CO.
1894.

Oxford
HORACE HART, PRINTER TO THE UNIVERSITY

CONTENTS.

—••—

Out of the Deep have I called unto Thee,

    O Lord 5

Christ our All in all 17

Some Feasts and Fasts 49

Gifts and Graces 99

The World. Self-Destruction. . . . 119

Divers Worlds. Time and Eternity . . 127

New Jerusalem and its Citizens . . 149

Songs for Strangers and Pilgrims . . 171

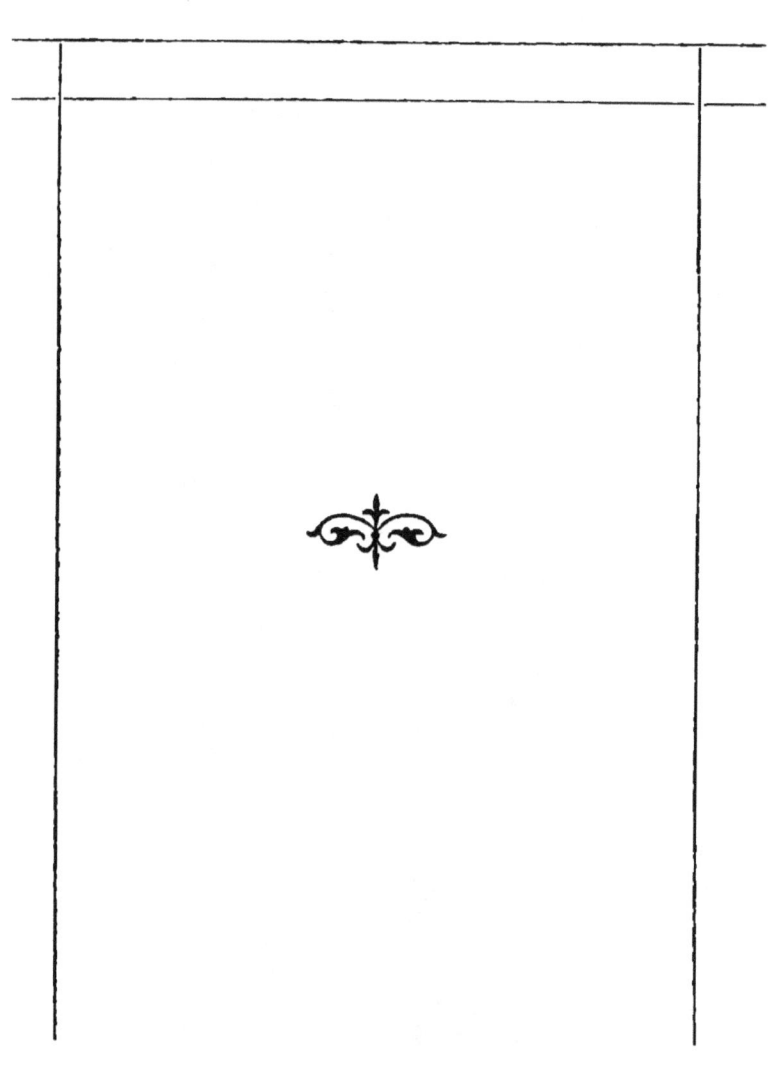

*"OUT OF THE DEEP HAVE
I CALLED UNTO THEE,
O LORD."*

Verses.

"OUT OF THE DEEP HAVE I CALLED UNTO THEE, O LORD."

—•—

ALONE Lord God, in Whom our trust and
      peace,
  Our love and our desire, glow bright with hope;
  Lift us above this transitory scope
Of earth, these pleasures that begin and cease,
This moon which wanes, these seasons which
      decrease:
  We turn to Thee; as on an eastern slope
  Wheat feels the dawn beneath night's lingering
      cope,
Bending and stretching sunward ere it sees.
Alone Lord God, we see not yet we know;
  By love we dwell with patience and desire,
    And loving so and so desiring pray;
    Thy Will be done in earth as heaven to-day;
As yesterday it was, tomorrow so;
  Love offering love on love's self-feeding fire.

"Out of the Deep have I called

SEVEN vials hold Thy wrath: but what can hold
    Thy mercy save Thine own Infinitude
    Boundlessly overflowing with all good,
All lovingkindness, all delights untold?
Thy Love, of each created love the mould;
    Thyself, of all the empty plenitude;
    Heard of at Ephrata, found in the Wood,
For ever One, the Same, and Manifold.
Lord, give us grace to tremble with that dove
    Which Ark-bound winged its solitary way
    And overpast the Deluge in a day,
        Whom Noah's hand pulled in and comforted:
For we who much more hang upon Thy Love
    Behold its shadow in the deed he did.

"Where neither rust nor moth doth corrupt."

NERVE us with patience, Lord, to toil or rest,
    Toiling at rest on our allotted level;
    Unsnared, unscared by world or flesh or devil,
Fulfilling the good Will of Thy behest:
    Not careful here to hoard, not here to revel;
But waiting for our treasure and our zest
Beyond the fading splendour of the west,
    Beyond this deathstruck life and deathlier evil.
Not with the sparrow building here a house:
    But with the swallow tabernacling so
    As still to poise alert to rise and go
        On eager wings with wing-outspeeding wills
Beyond earth's gourds and past her almond boughs,
    Past utmost bound of the everlasting hills.

"As the sparks fly upwards."

LORD, grant us wills to trust Thee with such aim
  Of hope and passionate craving of desire,
That we may mount aspiring, and aspire
Still while we mount; rejoicing in Thy Name
Yesterday, this day, day by day the Same:
 So sparks fly upward scaling heaven by fire,
 Still mount and still attain not, yet draw nigher
While they have being to their fountain flame.
To saints who mount, the bottomless abyss
 Is as mere nothing, they have set their face
 Onward and upward toward that blessèd place
  Where man rejoices with his God, and soul
With soul, in the unutterable kiss
  Of peace for every victor at the goal.

LORD, make us all love all: that when we meet
  Even myriads of earth's myriads at Thy Bar,
  We may be glad as all true lovers are
Who having parted count reunion sweet.
Safe gathered home around Thy blessèd Feet,
 Come home by different roads from near or far,
 Whether by whirlwind or by flaming car,
From pangs or sleep, safe folded round Thy seat.
Oh, if our brother's blood cry out at us,
 How shall we meet Thee Who hast loved us all,
  Thee Whom we never loved, not loving him?
  The unloving cannot chant with Seraphim,
Bear harp of gold or palm victorious,
  Or face the Vision Beatifical.

"Out of the Deep have I called

LORD, I am ashamed to seek Thy Face
        As tho' I loved Thee as Thy saints love
        Thee:
        Yet turn from those Thy lovers, look on me,
Disgrace me not with uttermost disgrace;
But pour on me ungracious, pour Thy grace
        To purge my heart and bid my will go free,
        Till I too taste Thy hidden Sweetness, see
Thy hidden Beauty in the holy place.
O Thou Who callest sinners to repent,
        Call me Thy sinner unto penitence,
                For many sins grant me the greater love:
                Set me above the waterfloods, above
        Devil and shifting world and fleshly sense,
Thy Mercy's all-amazing monument.

IT is not death, O Christ, to die for Thee:
        Nor is that silence of a silent land
Which speaks Thy praise so all may understand:
Darkness of death makes Thy dear lovers see
Thyself Who Wast and Art and Art to Be;
        Thyself, more lovely than the lovely band
        Of saints who worship Thee on either hand,
Loving and loved thro' all eternity.
Death is not death, and therefore do I hope:
        Nor silence silence; and I therefore sing
                A very humble hopeful quiet psalm,
                Searching my heart-field for an offering;
        A handful of sun-courting heliotrope,
                Of myrrh a bundle, and a little balm.

LORD, grant us eyes to see and ears to hear,
    And souls to love and minds to understand,
    And steadfast faces toward the Holy Land,
And confidence of hope, and filial fear,
And citizenship where Thy saints appear
    Before Thee heart in heart and hand in hand,
    And Alleluias where their chanting band
As waters and as thunders fill the sphere.
Lord, grant us what Thou wilt, and what Thou wilt
    Deny, and fold us in Thy peaceful fold:
      Not as the world gives, give to us Thine own:
Inbuild us where Jerusalem is built
    With walls of jasper and with streets of gold,
      And Thou Thyself, Lord Christ, for Corner
      Stone.

" Cried out with Tears."

LORD, I believe, help Thou mine unbelief:
    Lord, I repent, help mine impenitence:
    Hide not Thy Face from me, nor spurn me hence,
Nor utterly despise me in my grief;
Nor say me nay, who worship with the thief
    Bemoaning my so long lost innocence:—
    Ah me! my penitence a fresh offence,
Too tardy and too tepid and too brief.
Lord, must I perish, I who look to Thee?
    Look Thou upon me, bid me live, not die;
      Say " Come," say not " Depart," tho' Thou
      art just:
      Yea, Lord, be mindful how out of the dust
I look to Thee while Thou dost look on me,
    Thou Face to face with me and Eye to eye.

LORD, on Whom we gaze and dare not gaze,
   Increase our faith that gazing we may see,
   And seeing love, and loving worship Thee
Thro' all our days, our long and lengthening days.
O Lord, accessible to prayer and praise,
   Kind Lord, Companion of the two or three,
   Good Lord, be gracious to all men and me,
Lighten our darkness and amend our ways.
Call up our hearts to Thee, that where Thou art
   Our treasure and our heart may dwell at one:
   Then let the pallid moon pursue her sun,
So long as it shall please Thee, far apart,—
   Yet art Thou with us, Thou to Whom we run,
We hand in hand with Thee and heart in heart.

"I will come and heal him."

LORD God, hear the silence of each soul,
   Its cry unutterable of ruth and shame,
   Its voicelessness of self-contempt and blame:
Nor suffer harp and palm and aureole
Of multitudes who praise Thee at the goal,
   To set aside Thy poor and blind and lame;
   Nor blazing Seraphs utterly to outflame
The spark that flies up from each earthly coal.
My price Thy priceless Blood; and therefore I
   Price of Thy priceless Blood am precious so
     That good things love me in their love of Thee:
     I comprehend not why Thou lovedst me
   With Thy so mighty Love; but this I know,
No man hath greater love than thus to die.

AH Lord, Lord, if my heart were right with
  Thine
  As Thine with mine, then should I rest resigned
  Awaiting knowledge with a quiet mind
Because of heavenly wisdom's anodyne.
Then would Thy Love be more to me than wine,
  Then should I seek being sure at length to find,
  Then should I trust to Thee all humankind
Because Thy Love of them is more than mine.
Then should I stir up hope and comfort me
  Remembering Thy Cradle and Thy Cross;
  How Heaven to Thee without us had been loss,
  How Heaven with us is Thy one only Heaven,
Heaven shared with us thro' all eternity,
  With us long sought, long loved, and much
    forgiven.

❖

"The gold of that land is good."

I LONG for joy, O Lord, I long for gold,
  I long for all Thou profferest to me,
I long for the unimagined manifold
  Abundance laid up in Thy treasury.
  I long for pearls, but not from mundane sea;
I long for palms, but not from earthly mould;
  Yet in all else I long for, long for Thee,
Thyself to hear and worship and behold.
For Thee, beyond the splendour of that day
  Where all is day and is not any night;
  For Thee, beyond refreshment of that rest
  To which tired saints press on for its delight :—
Or if not thus for Thee, yet Thee I pray
  To make me long so till Thou make me blest

WEIGH all my faults and follies righteously,
    Omissions and commissions, sin on sin;
  Make deep the scale, O Lord, to weigh them in;
Yea, set the Accuser vulture-eyed to see
All loads ingathered which belong to me:
    That so in life the judgement may begin,
    And Angels learn how hard it is to win
One solitary sinful soul to Thee.
I have no merits for a counterpoise:
    Oh vanity my work and hastening day,
What can I answer to the accusing voice?
    Lord, drop Thou in the counterscale alone
    One Drop from Thine own Heart, and overweigh
    My guilt, my folly, even my heart of stone.

LORD, grant me grace to love Thee in my pain,
    Thro' all my disappointment love Thee still,
  Thy love my strong foundation and my hill,
'Tho' I be such as cometh not again,
A fading leaf, a spark upon the wane:
    So evermore do Thou Thy perfect Will
    Beloved thro' all my good, thro' all mine ill,
Beloved tho' all my love beside be vain.
If thus I love Thee, how wilt Thou love me,
    Thou Who art greater than my heart? (Amen!)
    Wilt Thou bestow a part, withhold a part?
The longing of my heart cries out to Thee,
    The hungering thirsting longing of my heart:
    What I forewent wilt Thou not grant me then?

LORD, make me one with Thine own faithful
ones,
Thy Saints who love Thee and are loved by Thee;
Till the day break and till the shadows flee,
At one with them in alms and orisons;
At one with him who toils and him who runs,
And him who yearns for union yet to be;
At one with all who throng the crystal sea
And wait the setting of our moons and suns.
Ah, my beloved ones gone on before,
Who looked not back with hand upon the plough!
If beautiful to me while still in sight,
How beautiful must be your aspects now;
Your unknown, well-known aspects in that light
Which clouds shall never cloud for evermore.

"Light of Light."

CHRIST our Light, Whom even in darkness we
(So we look up) discern and gaze upon,
O Christ, Thou loveliest Light that ever shone,
Thou Light of Light, Fount of all lights that be,
Grant us clear vision of Thy Light to see,
Tho' other lights elude us, or begone
Into the secret of oblivion,
Or gleam in places higher than man's degree.
Who looks on Thee looks full on his desire,
Who looks on Thee looks full on Very Love:
Looking, he answers well, "What lack I yet?"
His heat and cold wait not on earthly fire,
His wealth is not of earth to lose or get;
Earth reels, but he has stored his store above.

CHRIST OUR ALL IN ALL.

"The ransomed of the Lord."

THY lovely saints do bring Thee love,
   Incense and joy and gold;
Fair star with star, fair dove with dove,
   Beloved by Thee of old.
I, Master, neither star nor dove,
   Have brought Thee sins and tears;
Yet I too bring a little love
   Amid my flaws and fears.
A trembling love that faints and fails
   Yet still is love of Thee,
A wondering love that hopes and hails
   Thy boundless Love of me;
Love kindling faith and pure desire,
   Love following on to bliss,
A spark, O Jesu, from Thy fire,
   A drop from Thine abyss.

LORD, we are rivers running to Thy sea,
    Our waves and ripples all derived from Thee:
A nothing we should have, a nothing be,
    Except for Thee.

Sweet are the waters of Thy shoreless sea,
Make sweet our waters that make haste to Thee;
Pour in Thy sweetness, that ourselves may be
    Sweetness to Thee.

"An exceeding bitter cry."

CONTEMPT and pangs and haunting fears—
    Too late for hope, too late for ease,
      Too late for rising from the dead;
    Too late, too late to bend my knees,
      Or bow my head,
Or weep, or ask for tears.

Hark! . . . One I hear Who calls to me:
    "Give Me thy thorn and grief and scorn,
      Give Me thy ruin and regret.
    Press on thro' darkness toward the morn:
      One loves thee yet:
Have I forgotten thee?"

Lord, Who art Thou? Lord, is it Thou
    My Lord and God Lord Jesus Christ?
      How said I that I sat alone
    And desolate and unsufficed?
      Surely a stone
Would raise Thy praises now!

Christ our All in all.

LORD, when Thou didst call me, didst Thou
      know
  My heart disheartened thro' and thro',
  Still hankering after Egypt full in view
Where cucumbers and melons grow?
                    —" Yea, I knew."—

But, Lord, when Thou didst choose me, didst Thou
      know
  How marred I was and withered too,
  Nor rose for sweetness nor for virtue rue,
Timid and rash, hasty and slow?
                    —" Yea, I knew." —

My Lord, when Thou didst love me, didst Thou
      know
  How weak my efforts were, how few,
  Tepid to love and impotent to do,
Envious to reap while slack to sow?
                    —" Yea, I knew."—

Good Lord, Who knowest what I cannot know
  And dare not know, my false, my true,
  My new, my old; Good Lord, arise and do
If loving Thou hast known me so.
                    —" Yea, I knew."—

Christ our All in all.

"Thou, God, seest me."

AH me, that I should be
  Exposed and open evermore to Thee!—
"Nay, shrink not from My light,
And I will make thee glorious in My sight
With the overcoming Shulamite."—
Yea, Lord, Thou moulding me.

. . . Without a hiding-place
To hide me from the terrors of Thy Face.—
"Thy hiding-place is here
In Mine own heart, wherefore the Roman spear
For thy sake I accounted dear."—
My Jesus! King of Grace.

. . . Without a veil, to give
Whiteness before Thy Face that I might live.—
"Am I too poor to dress
Thee in My royal robe of righteousness?
Challenge and prove My Love's excess."—
Give, Lord, I will receive.

. . . Without a pool wherein
To wash my piteous self and make me clean.—
"My Blood hath washed away
Thy guilt, and still I wash thee day by day:
Only take heed to trust and pray."—
Lord, help me to begin.

✤

Christ our All in all.

LORD Jesus, who would think that I am Thine?
  Ah, who would think
Who sees me ready to turn back or sink,
  That Thou art mine?

I cannot hold Thee fast tho' Thou art mine:
  Hold Thou me fast,
So earth shall know at last and heaven at last
  That I am Thine.

"The Name of Jesus."

JESUS, Lord God from all eternity,
  Whom love of us brought down to shame,
I plead Thy Life with Thee,
  I plead Thy Death, I plead Thy Name.

Jesus, Lord God of every living soul,
  Thy Love exceeds its uttered fame,
Thy Will can make us whole,
  I plead Thyself, I plead Thy Name.

LORD God of Hosts, most Holy and most High,
  What made Thee tell Thy Name of Love
      to me?
What made Thee live our life? what made Thee
      die?
  "My love of thee."

I pitched so low, Thou so exceeding high,
  What was it made Thee stoop to look at me
While flawless sons of God stood wondering by?
    " My love of thee."

What is there which can lift me up on high
  That we may dwell together. Thou with me,
When sin and death and suffering are gone by?
    " My love of thee."

O Lord, what is that best thing hid on high
Which makes heaven heaven as Thou hast pro-
    mised me,
Yea, makes it Christ to live and gain to die?
    " My love of thee."

LORD, what have I that I may offer Thee?
    Look, Lord, I pray Thee, and see.—
What is it thou hast got?
Nay, child, what is it thou hast not?
Thou hast all gifts that I have given to thee:
Offer them all to Me,
The great ones and the small,
I will accept them one and all.—

I have a will, good Lord, but it is marred;
A heart both crushed and hard:
Not such as these the gift
Clean-handed lovely saints uplift.—

Nay, child, but wilt thou judge for Me?
I crave not thine, but thee.—

Ah, Lord, Who lovest me!
Such as I have now give I Thee.

Christ our All in all.

F I should say "my heart is in my home,"
 I turn away from that high halidom
Where Jesus sits: for nowhere else
But with its treasure dwells
The heart: this Truth and this experience tells.

If I should say "my heart is in a grave,"
I turn away from Jesus risen to save:
 I slight that death He died for me;
 I, too, deny to see
His beauty and desirability.

O Lord, Whose Heart is deeper than my heart,
Draw mine to Thine to worship where Thou art;
 For Thine own glory join the twain
 Never to part again,
Nor to have lived nor to have died in vain.

EAF from leaf Christ knows;
 Himself the Lily and the Rose:

Sheep from sheep Christ tells;
Himself the Shepherd, no one else:

Star and star He names,
Himself outblazing all their flames:

Dove by dove, He calls
To set each on the golden walls:

Drop by drop, He counts
The flood of ocean as it mounts:

Grain by grain, His hand
Numbers the innumerable sand.

Lord, I lift to Thee
In peace what is and what shall be :

Lord, in peace I trust
To Thee all spirits and all dust.

LORD, carry me. —Nay, but I grant thee
strength
To walk and work thy way to Heaven at length.—

Lord, why then am I weak?—Because I give
Power to the weak, and bid the dying live.—

Lord, I am tired.—He hath not much desired
The goal, who at the starting-point is tired.—

Lord, dost Thou know?—I know what is in man;
What the flesh can, and what the spirit can.—

Lord, dost Thou care?—Yea, for thy gain or loss
So much I cared, it brought Me to the Cross.—

Lord, I believe; help Thou mine unbelief.—
Good is the word; but rise, for life is brief.

The follower is not greater than the Chief:
Follow thou Me along My way of grief.

Christ our All in all.

LORD, I am here.—But, child, I look for thee
        Elsewhere and nearer Me.—
Lord, that way moans a wide insatiate sea:
        How can I come to Thee?—
Set foot upon the water, test and see
        If thou canst come to Me.—
Couldst Thou not send a boat to carry me,
        Or dolphin swimming free?—
Nay, boat nor fish if thy will faileth thee:
        For My Will too is free.—
O Lord, I am afraid.—Take hold on Me:
        I am stronger than the sea.—
Save, Lord, I perish.—I have hold of thee,
        I made and rule the sea,
I bring thee to the haven where thou wouldst be.

NEW creatures; the Creator still the Same
        For ever and for ever: therefore we
Win hope from God's unsearchable decree
And glorify His still unchanging Name.
We too are still the same: and still our claim,
        Our trust, our stay, is Jesus, none but He:
        He still the Same regards us, and still we
Mount toward Him in old love's accustomed flame.
We know Thy wounded Hands: and Thou dost
                know
        Our praying hands, our hands that clasp and cling
To hold Thee fast and not to let Thee go.
        All else be new then, Lord, as Thou hast said:
        Since it is Thou, we dare not be afraid,
        Our King of old and still our Self-same King.

Christ our All in all.

"King of kings and Lord of lords."

IS this that Name as ointment poured forth
   For which the virgins love Thee; King of
      kings
And Lord of lords? All Seraphs clad in wings;
All Cherubs and all Wheels which south and north,
Which east and west turn not in going forth;
   All many-semblanced ordered Spirits, as rings
   Of rainbow in unwonted fashionings,
Might answer, Yes. But we from south and north,
From east and west, a feeble folk who came
   By desert ways in quest of land unseen,
   A promised land of pasture ever green
   And ever springing ever singing wave,
Know best Thy Name of Jesus: Blessed Name,
   Man's life and resurrection from the grave.

THY Name, O Christ, as incense streaming forth
   Sweetens our names before God's Holy Face;
Luring us from the south and from the north
   Unto the sacred place.

In Thee God's promise is Amen and Yea.
   What art Thou to us? Prize of every lot,
Shepherd and Door, our Life and Truth and Way:—
   Nay, Lord, what art Thou not?

"The Good Shepherd."

SHEPHERD with the bleeding Feet,
  Good Shepherd with the pleading Voice,
    What seekest Thou from hill to hill?
Sweet were the valley pastures, sweet
  The sound of flocks that bleat their joys,
    And eat and drink at will.
Is one worth seeking, when Thou hast of Thine
        Ninety and nine? —

How should I stay my bleeding Feet,
  How should I hush my pleading Voice?
    I Who chose death and clomb a hill,
Accounting gall and wormwood sweet,
  That hundredfold might bud My joys
    For love's sake and good will.
I seek My one, for all there bide of Mine
        Ninety and nine.

"Rejoice with Me."

LITTLE Lamb, who lost thee? —
  I myself, none other.—
Little Lamb, who found thee? —
  Jesus, Shepherd, Brother.
Ah, Lord, what I cost Thee!
  Canst Thou still desire? —
Still Mine arms surround thee,
  Still I lift thee higher,
  Draw thee nigher.

SHALL not the Judge of all the earth do
    right?
  Yea, Lord, altho' Thou say me nay:
Shall not His Will be to me life and light?
  Yea, Lord, altho' Thou slay.

Yet, Lord, remembering turn and sift and see,
  Remember tho' Thou sift me thro',
Remember my desire, remember me,
  Remember, Lord, and do.

ME and my gift: kind Lord, behold,
    Be not extreme to test or sift;
Thy Love can turn to fire and gold
  Me and my gift.

  Myself and mine to Thee I lift:
Gather us to Thee from the cold
  Dead outer world where dead things drift.

  If much were mine, then manifold
  Should be the offering of my thrift:
I am but poor, yet love makes bold
  Me and my gift.

"He cannot deny Himself."

LOVE still is Love, and doeth all things well,
Whether He show me heaven or hell
    Or earth in her decay
    Passing away
    On a day.

Love still is Love, tho' He should say, "Depart,"
And break my incorrigible heart,
    And set me out of sight
    Widowed of light
    In the night.

Love still is Love, is Love, if He should say,
"Come," on that uttermost dread day;
    "Come," unto very me,
    "Come where I be,
    Come and see."

Love still is Love, whatever comes to pass:
O Only Love, make me Thy glass,
    Thy pleasure to fulfil
    By loving still
    Come what will.

"Slain from the foundation of the world."

SLAIN for man, slain for me, O Lamb of
    God, look down;
Loving to the end look down, behold and see:
Turn Thine Eyes of pity, turn not on us Thy
    frown,
    O Lamb of God, slain for man, slain for me.

Mark the wrestling, mark the race for indeed
    a crown;
Mark our chariots how we drive them heavily;
Mark the foe upon our track blasting thundering
    down,
    O Lamb of God, slain for man, slain for me.

Set as a Cloudy Pillar against them Thy frown,
  Thy Face of Light toward us gracious utterly;
Help granting, hope granting, until Thou grant
    a crown,
    O Lamb of God, slain for man, slain for me.

LORD Jesu, Thou art sweetness to my soul:
    I to myself am bitterness:
Regard my fainting struggle toward the goal,
    Regard my manifold distress,
      O Sweet Jesu.

Thou art Thyself my goal, O Lord my King:
    Stretch forth Thy hand to save my soul:
What matters more or less of journeying?
    While I touch Thee I touch my goal,
      O Sweet Jesu.

O LORD, Thy foolish sinner low and small,
    Lack all.
His heart too high was set
Who asked, What lack I yet?
Woe's me at my most woeful pass!
I, Lord, who scarcely dare adore,
Weep sore:
Steeped in this rotten world I fear to rot.
Alas! what lack I not?
Alas! alas for me! alas
More and yet more!—

Nay, stand up on thy feet, betaking thee
To Me.
Bring fear; but much more bring
Hope to thy patient King:
What, is My pleasure in thy death?
I loved that youth who little knew
The true
Width of his want, yet worshipped with goodwill:
So love I thee, and still
Prolong thy day of grace and breath.
Rise up and do.—

Lord, let me know mine end, and certify
When I
Shall die and have to stand
Helpless on Either Hand,
Cut off, cut off, my day of grace.—
Not so: for what is that to thee?
I see
The measure and the number of thy day:
Keep patience, tho' I slay;
Keep patience till thou see My Face.
Follow thou Me.

"Because He first loved us."

I WAS hungry, and Thou feddest me;
   Yea, Thou gavest drink to slake my thirst:
O Lord, what love gift can I offer Thee
    Who hast loved me first?—

Christ our All in all.

Feed My hungry brethren for My sake;
  Give them drink, for love of them and Me:
Love them as I loved thee, when Bread I brake
    In pure love of thee.—

Yea, Lord, I will serve them by Thy grace;
  Love Thee, seek Thee, in them; wait and pray:
Yet would I love Thyself, Lord, face to face,
    Heart to heart, one day.—

Let today fulfil its daily task,
  Fill thy heart and hand to them and Me:
Tomorrow thou shalt ask, and shalt not ask
    Half I keep for thee.

LORD, hast Thou so loved us, and will not we
    Love Thee with heart and mind and
        strength and soul,
  Desiring Thee beyond our glorious goal,
Beyond the heaven of heavens desiring Thee?
Each saint, all saints cry out: Yea me, yea me,
    Thou hast desired beyond an aureole,
    Beyond Thy many Crowns, beyond the whole
Ninety and nine unwandering family.
Souls in green pastures of the watered land,
Faint pilgrim souls wayfaring thro' the sand,
    Abide with Thee and in Thee are at rest:
    Yet evermore, kind Lord, renew Thy quest
After new wanderers; such as once Thy Hand
    Gathered, Thy Shoulders bore, Thy Heart
        caressed.

Christ our All in all.

AS the dove which found no rest
For the sole of her foot, flew back
To the ark her only nest
And found safety there;
Because Noah put forth his hand,
Drew her in from ruin and wrack,
And was more to her than the land
And the air:

So my spirit, like that dove,
Fleeth away to an ark
Where dwelleth a Heart of Love,
A Hand pierced to save,
Tho' the sun and the moon should fail,
Tho' the stars drop into the dark,
And my body lay itself pale
In a grave.

"Thou art Fairer than the children of men."

A ROSE, a lily, and the Face of Christ
Have all our hearts sufficed:
For He is Rose of Sharon nobly born,
Our Rose without a thorn;
And He is Lily of the Valley, He
Most sweet in purity.
But when we come to name Him as He is,
Godhead, Perfection, Bliss,
All tongues fall silent, while pure hearts alone
Complete their orison.

"As the Apple Tree among the trees of the wood."

AS one red rose in a garden where all other
    roses are white
Blossoms alone in its glory, crowned all alone
In a solitude of own sweetness and fragrance of
    own delight,
With loveliness not another's and thorns its own ;
As one ruddy sun amid million orbs comely and
    colourless,
Among all others, above all others is known ;
As it were alone in the garden, alone in the
    heavenly place,
Chief and centre of all, in fellowship yet alone.

NONE other Lamb, none other Name,
    None other Hope in heaven or earth or sea,
None other Hiding-place from guilt and shame,
    None beside Thee.

My faith burns low, my hope burns low,
    Only my heart's desire cries out in me
By the deep thunder of its want and woe,
    Cries out to Thee.

Lord, Thou art Life tho' I be dead,
    Love's Fire Thou art however cold I be:
Nor heaven have I, nor place to lay my head,
    Nor home, but Thee.

"Thy Friend and thy Father's Friend forget not."

FRIENDS, I commend to you the narrow way:
 Not because I, please God, will walk therein,
But rather for the Love Feast of that day,
The exceeding prize which whoso will may win.
 Earth is half spent and rotting at the core,
 Here hollow death's heads mock us with a grin,
Here heartiest laughter leaves us tired and sore.
 Men heap up pleasures and enlarge desire,
 Outlive desire, and famished evermore
Consume themselves within the undying fire.
 Yet not for this God made us: not for this
 Christ sought us far and near to draw us nigher,
Sought us and found and paid our penalties.
 If one could answer "Nay" to God's command,
 Who shall say "Nay" when Christ pleads all He is
For us, and holds us with a wounded Hand?

"Surely He hath borne our griefs."

CHRIST'S Heart was wrung for me, if mine is sore;
 And if my feet are weary, His have bled;
 He had no place wherein to lay His Head;
If I am burdened, He was burdened more.
The cup I drink, He drank of long before;
 He felt the unuttered anguish which I dread;
 He hungered Who the hungry thousands fed,
And thirsted Who the world's refreshment bore.

Christ our All in all.

If grief be such a looking-glass as shows
    Christ's Face and man's in some sort made alike,
      Then grief is pleasure with a subtle taste:
      Wherefore should any fret or faint or haste?
Grief is not grievous to a soul that knows
    Christ comes,—and listens for that hour to strike.

"They toil not, neither do they spin."

CLOTHER of the lily, Feeder of the sparrow,
  Father of the fatherless, dear Lord,
Tho' Thou set me as a mark against Thine arrow,
  As a prey unto Thy sword,
As a ploughed up field beneath Thy harrow,
  As a captive in Thy cord,   [narrow
Let that cord be love; and some day make my
  Hallowed bed according to Thy Word. Amen.

DARKNESS and light are both alike to Thee:
  Therefore to Thee I lift my darkened face;
Upward I look with eyes that fail to see,
  Athirst for future light and present grace.
I trust the Hand of Love I scarcely trace.
  With breath that fails I cry, Remember me:
  Add breath to breath, so I may run my race
That where Thou art there may Thy servant be.
For Thou art gulf and fountain of my love,
  I unreturning torrent to Thy sea,
    Yea, Thou the measureless ocean for my rill:
    Seeking I find, and finding seek Thee still:
And oh! that I had wings as hath a dove,
  Then would I flee away to rest with Thee.

Christ our All in all.

"And now why tarriest thou?"

LORD, grant us grace to mount by steps of grace
From grace to grace nearer, my God, to
Thee;
Not tarrying for tomorrow,
Lest we lie down in sorrow
And never see
Unveiled Thy Face.

Life is a vapour vanishing in haste;
Life is a day whose sun grows pale to set;
Life is a stint and sorrow,
One day and not the morrow;
Precious, while yet
It runs to waste.

Lord, strengthen us; lest fainting by the way
We come not to Thee, we who come from far;
Lord, bring us to that morrow
Which makes an end of sorrow,
Where all saints are
On holyday.

Where all the saints rest who have heard Thy call,
Have risen and striven and now rejoice in rest:
Call us too home from sorrow
To rest in Thee tomorrow;
In Thee our Best,
In Thee our All.

HAVE I not striven, my God, and watched
    and prayed?
Have I not wrestled in mine agony?
Wherefore still turn Thy Face of Grace from me?
Is Thine Arm shortened that Thou canst not aid?
Thy silence breaks my heart: speak tho' to upbraid,
    For Thy rebuke yet bids us follow Thee.
I grope and grasp not; gaze, but cannot see.
When out of sight and reach my bed is made,
And piteous men and women cease to blame
    Whispering and wistful of my gain or loss;
    Thou Who for my sake once didst feel the Cross,
      Lord, wilt Thou turn and look upon me then,
And in Thy Glory bring to nought my shame,
    Confessing me to angels and to men?

"God is our Hope and Strength."

TEMPEST and terror below; but Christ the
    Almighty above.
    Tho' the depth of the deep overflow, tho' fire
      run along on the ground,
Tho' all billows and flames make a noise,—and
      where is an Ark for the dove?—
    Tho' sorrows rejoice against joys, and death
      and destruction abound:
Yet Jesus abolisheth death, and Jesus Who loves
      us we love;
    His dead are renewed with a breath, His lost
      are the sought and the found.

Thy wanderers call and recall, Thy dead men
    lift out of the ground;
  O Jesus, Who lovest us all, stoop low from
    Thy Glory above:
Where sin hath abounded make grace to abound
    and to superabound,
  Till we gaze on Thee face unto Face, and re-
    spond to Thee love unto Love.

DAY and night the Accuser makes no pause,
    Day and night protest the Righteous Laws,
Good and Evil witness to man's flaws;
Man the culprit, man's the ruined cause,
Man midway to death's devouring jaws
  And the worm that gnaws.

Day and night our Jesus makes no pause,
Pleads His own fulfilment of all laws,
Veils with His Perfections mortal flaws,
Clears the culprit, pleads the desperate cause,
Plucks the dead from death's devouring jaws
  And the worm that gnaws.

MINE enemy
    Rejoice not over me!
  Jesus waiteth to be gracious:
    I will yet arise,
Mounting free and far,
Past sun and star,
    To a house prepared and spacious
    In the skies.

Lord, for Thine own sake
Kindle my heart and break;
  Make mine anguish efficacious
  Wedded to Thine own:
Be not Thy dear pain,
Thy Love in vain,
  Thou Who waitest to be gracious
  On Thy Throne.

LORD, dost Thou look on me, and will not I
  Launch out my heart to Heaven to look
    on Thee?
Here if one loved me I should turn to see,
And often think on him and often sigh,
And by a tender friendship make reply
  To love gratuitous poured forth on me,
And nurse a hope of happy days to be,
And mean "until we meet" in each good-bye.
Lord, Thou dost look and love is in Thine Eyes,
  Thy heart is set upon me day and night,
    Thou stoopest low to set me far above:
O Lord, that I may love Thee make me wise;
  That I may see and love Thee grant me sight;
    And give me love that I may give Thee love.

"Peace I leave with you."

TUMULT and turmoil, trouble and toil,
  Yet peace withal in a painful heart;
Never a grudge and never a broil,
  And ever the better part.

Christ our All in all.

O my King and my heart's own choice,
  Stretch Thy Hand to Thy fluttering dove;
Teach me, call to me with Thy Voice,
  Wrap me up in Thy Love.

CHRIST our All in each, our All in all!
  Others have this or that, a love, a friend,
A trusted teacher, a long worked for end:
But what to me were Peter or were Paul
  Without Thee? fame or friend if such might be?
  Thee wholly will I love, Thee wholly seek,
Follow Thy foot-track, hearken for Thy call.
  O Christ mine All in all, my flesh is weak,
A trembling fawning tyrant unto me:
  Turn, look upon me, let me hear Thee speak:
Tho' bitter billows of Thine utmost sea
Swathe me, and darkness build around its wall,
Yet will I rise, Thou lifting when I fall,
  And if Thou hold me fast, yet cleave to Thee.

BECAUSE Thy Love hath sought me,
  All mine is Thine and Thine is mine:
Because Thy Blood hath bought me,
  I will not be mine own but Thine.

I lift my heart to Thy Heart,
  Thy Heart sole resting-place for mine:
Shall Thy Heart crave for my heart,
  And shall not mine crave back for Thine?

Christ our All in all.

THY fainting spouse, yet still Thy spouse;
  Thy trembling dove, yet still Thy dove;
Thine own by mutual vows,
  By mutual love.

Recall Thy vows, if not her vows;
  Recall Thy Love, if not her love:
For weak she is, Thy spouse,
  And tired, Thy dove.

"Like as the hart desireth the water brooks."

MY heart is yearning:
    Behold my yearning heart,
  And lean low to satisfy
  Its lonely beseeching cry,
    For Thou its fulness art.

Turn, as once turning
    Thou didst behold Thy Saint
    In deadly extremity;
    Didst look, and win back to Thee
  His will frighted and faint.

Kindle my burning
    From Thine unkindled Fire;
    Fill me with gifts and with grace
    That I may behold Thy Face,
  For Thee I desire.

My heart is yearning,
    Yearning and thrilling thro'
    For Thy Love mine own of old,
    For Thy Love unknown, untold,
  Ever old, ever new.

Christ our All in all.

"That where I am, there ye may be also."

HOW know I that it looms lovely that land
I have never seen,
With morning-glories and heartsease and unex-
ampled green,
With neither heat nor cold in the balm-redolent
air?
Some of this, not all, I know; but this is so;
Christ is there.

How know I that blessedness befalls who dwell
in Paradise,
The outwearied hearts refreshing, rekindling the
worn-out eyes,
All souls singing, seeing, rejoicing everywhere?
Nay, much more than this I know; for this is so;
Christ is there.

O Lord Christ, Whom having not seen I love and
desire to love,
O Lord Christ, Who lookest on me uncomely yet
still Thy dove,
Take me to Thee in Paradise, Thine own made
fair;
For whatever else I know, this thing is so;
Thou art there.

"Judge not according to the appearance."

LORD, purge our eyes to see
  Within the seed a tree,
Within the glowing egg a bird,
  Within the shroud a butterfly:

Till taught by such, we see
Beyond all creatures Thee,
  And hearken for Thy tender word,
  And hear it, "Fear not: it is I."

MY God, wilt Thou accept, and will not we
  Give aught to Thee?
The kept we lose, the offered we retain
  Or find again.

Yet if our gift were lost, we well might lose
  All for Thy use:
Well lost for Thee, Whose love is all for us
  Gratuitous.

A CHILL blank world. Yet over the utmost
  sea
The light of a coming dawn is rising to me,
  No more than a paler shade of darkness as yet;
While I lift my heart, O Lord, my heart unto Thee
  Who hast not forgotten me, yea, Who wilt not
    forget.

Christ our All in all.

Forget not Thy sorrowful servant, O Lord my God,
Weak as I cry, faint as I cry underneath Thy rod,
   Soon to lie dumb before Thee a body devoid
     of breath,
Dust to dust, ashes to ashes, a sod to the sod :
   Forget not my life, O my Lord, forget not my
     death.

❖

"The Chiefest among ten thousand."

JESU, better than Thy gifts
   Art Thou Thine only Self to us!
Palm branch its triumph, harp uplifts
   Its triumph-note melodious :
     But what are such to such as we ?
O Jesu, better than Thy saints
   Art Thou Thine only Self to us!
The heart faints and the spirit faints
   For only Thee all-Glorious,
     For Thee, O only Lord, for Thee.

SOME FEASTS AND FASTS.

SOME FEASTS AND FASTS.

ADVENT SUNDAY.

BEHOLD, the Bridegroom cometh: go ye out
With lighted lamps and garlands round about
To meet Him in a rapture with a shout.

It may be at the midnight, black as pitch,
Earth shall cast up her poor, cast up her rich.

It may be at the crowing of the cock
Earth shall upheave her depth, uproot her rock.

For lo, the Bridegroom fetcheth home the Bride:
His Hands are Hands she knows, she knows His
    Side.

Like pure Rebekah at the appointed place,
Veiled, she unveils her face to meet His Face.

Like great Queen Esther in her triumphing,
She triumphs in the Presence of her King.

His Eyes are as a Dove's, and she's Dove-eyed;
He knows His lovely mirror, sister, Bride.

He speaks with Dove-voice of exceeding love,
And she with love-voice of an answering Dove.

Behold, the Bridegroom cometh : go we out
With lamps ablaze and garlands round about
To meet Him in a rapture with a shout.

ADVENT.

EARTH grown old, yet still so green,
    Deep beneath her crust of cold
Nurses fire unfelt, unseen:
    Earth grown old.

    We who live are quickly told:
Millions more lie hid between
    Inner swathings of her fold.

When will fire break up her screen?
    When will life burst thro' her mould?
Earth, earth, earth, thy cold is keen,
    Earth grown old.

SOONER or later: yet at last
    The Jordan must be past;

It may be he will overflow
His banks the day we go;

It may be that his cloven deep
Will stand up on a heap.

Some Feasts and Fasts.

Sooner or later: yet one day
We all must pass that way;

Each man, each woman, humbled, pale,
Pass veiled within the veil;

Child, parent, bride, companion,
Alone, alone, alone.

For none a ransom can be paid,
A suretyship be made:

I, bent by mine own burden, must
Enter my house of dust;

I, rated to the full amount,
Must render mine account.

When earth and sea shall empty all
Their graves of great and small;

When earth wrapped in a fiery flood
Shall no more hide her blood;

When mysteries shall be revealed;
All secrets be unsealed;

When things of night, when things of shame,
Shall find at last a name,

Pealed for a hissing and a curse
Throughout the universe:

Then Awful Judge, most Awful God,
Then cause to bud Thy rod,

To bloom with blossoms, and to give
Almonds; yea, bid us live.

I plead Thyself with Thee, I plead
Thee in our utter need:

Jesus, most Merciful of Men,
Show mercy on us then;

Lord God of Mercy and of men,
Show mercy on us then.

CHRISTMAS EVE.

CHRISTMAS hath a darkness
   Brighter than the blazing noon,
Christmas hath a chillness
   Warmer than the heat of June,
Christmas hath a beauty
   Lovelier than the world can show:
For Christmas bringeth Jesus,
   Brought for us so low.

Earth, strike up your music,
   Birds that sing and bells that ring;
Heaven hath answering music
   For all Angels soon to sing:
Earth, put on your whitest
   Bridal robe of spotless snow:
For Christmas bringeth Jesus,
   Brought for us so low.

CHRISTMAS DAY.

A BABY is a harmless thing
   And wins our hearts with one accord,
And Flower of Babies was their King,
   Jesus Christ our Lord:
Lily of lilies He
Upon His Mother's knee;
Rose of roses, soon to be
Crowned with thorns on leafless tree.

A lamb is innocent and mild
   And merry on the soft green sod;
And Jesus Christ, the Undefiled,
   Is the Lamb of God:
Only spotless He
Upon His Mother's knee;
White and ruddy, soon to be
Sacrificed for you and me.

Nay, lamb is not so sweet a word,
   Nor lily half so pure a name;
Another name our hearts hath stirred,
   Kindling them to flame:
"Jesus" certainly
Is music and melody:
Heart with heart in harmony
Carol we and worship we.

CHRISTMASTIDE.

LOVE came down at Christmas,
 Love all lovely, Love Divine;
Love was born at Christmas,
 Star and Angels gave the sign.

Worship we the Godhead,
 Love Incarnate, Love Divine;
Worship we our Jesus:
 But wherewith for sacred sign?

Love shall be our token,
 Love be yours and love be mine,
Love to God and all men,
 Love for plea and gift and sign.

ST. JOHN, APOSTLE.

EARTH cannot bar flame from ascending,
 Hell cannot bind light from descending,
Death cannot finish life never ending.

Eagle and sun gaze at each other,
Eagle at sun, brother at Brother,
Loving in peace and joy one another.

O St. John, with chains for thy wages,
Strong thy rock where the storm-blast rages,
Rock of refuge, the Rock of Ages.

Rome hath passed with her awful voice,
Earth is passing with all her joys,
Heaven shall pass away with a noise.

So from us all follies that please us,
So from us all falsehoods that ease us,—
Only all saints abide with their Jesus.

Jesus, in love looking down hither,
Jesus, by love draw us up thither,
That we in Thee may abide together.

" ELOVED, let us love one another," says
St. John,
Eagle of eagles calling from above:
Words of strong nourishment for life to feed
upon,
"Beloved, let us love."

Voice of an eagle, yea, Voice of the Dove:
If we may love, winter is past and gone;
Publish we, praise we, for lo! it is enough.

More sunny than sunshine that ever yet shone,
Sweetener of the bitter, smoother of the rough,
Highest lesson of all lessons for all to con,
"Beloved, let us love."

HOLY INNOCENTS.

THEY scarcely waked before they slept,
They scarcely wept before they laughed;
They drank indeed death's bitter draught,
But all its bitterest dregs were kept
And drained by Mothers while they wept.

From Heaven the speechless Infants speak :
  Weep not (they say), our Mothers dear,
  For swords nor sorrows come not here.
Now we are strong who were so weak,
And all is ours we could not seek.

We bloom among the blooming flowers,
  We sing among the singing birds;
  Wisdom we have who wanted words:
Here morning knows not evening hours,
All's rainbow here without the showers.

And softer than our Mother's breast,
  And closer than our Mother's arm,
  Is here the Love that keeps us warm
And broods above our happy nest.
Dear Mothers, come: for Heaven is best.

UNSPOTTED lambs to follow the one Lamb,
  Unspotted doves to wait on the one Dove;
To whom Love saith, " Be with Me where I am,"
  And lo! their answer unto Love is love.

For tho' I know not any note they know,
  Nor know one word of all their song above,
I know Love speaks to them, and even so
  I know the answer unto Love is love.

EPIPHANY.

" LORD Babe, if Thou art He
      We sought for patiently,
Where is Thy court?
Hither may prophecy and star resort;
Men heed not their report."—
      "Bow down and worship, righteous man:
      This Infant of a span
      Is He man sought for since the world began!"—
"Then, Lord, accept my gold, too base a thing
For Thee, of all kings King."—

"Lord Babe, despite Thy youth
I hold Thee of a truth
Both Good and Great:
But wherefore dost Thou keep so mean a state,
Low-lying desolate?"—
      "Bow down and worship, righteous seer:
      The Lord our God is here
      Approachable, Who bids us all draw near."—
"Wherefore to Thee I offer frankincense,
Thou Sole Omnipotence."—

"But I have only brought
Myrrh; no wise afterthought
Instructed me
To gather pearls or gems, or choice to see
Coral or ivory."—
      "Not least thine offering proves thee wise:
      For myrrh means sacrifice,
      And He that lives, this Same is He that dies."—
"Then here is myrrh: alas! yea, woe is me
That myrrh befitteth Thee."—

Myrrh, frankincense, and gold:
And lo! from wintry fold
Good-will doth bring
A Lamb, the innocent likeness of this King
Whom stars and seraphs sing:
    And lo! the bird of love, a Dove
    Flutters and coos above:
    And Dove and Lamb and Babe agree in love:—
Come all mankind, come all creation hither,
Come, worship Christ together.

EPIPHANYTIDE.

TREMBLING before Thee we fall down to
    adore Thee,
  Shamefaced and trembling we lift our eyes to
    Thee :
O First and with the last! annul our ruined past,
  Rebuild us to Thy glory, set us free
  From sin and from sorrow to fall down and
    worship Thee.

Full of pity view us, stretch Thy sceptre to us,
  Bid us live that we may give ourselves to
    Thee :
O faithful Lord and True! stand up for us and do,
  Make us lovely, make us new, set us free—
  Heart and soul and spirit—to bring all and
    worship Thee.

Some Feasts and Fasts.

SEPTUAGESIMA.

"So run that ye may obtain."

ONE step more, and the race is ended;
One word more, and the lesson's done;
One toil more, and a long rest follows
At set of sun.

Who would fail, for one step withholden?
Who would fail, for one word unsaid?
Who would fail, for a pause too early?
Sound sleep the dead.

One step more, and the goal receives us;
One word more, and life's task is done;
One toil more, and the Cross is carried
And sets the sun.

SEXAGESIMA.

"Cursed is the ground for thy sake."

YET earth was very good in days of old,
And earth is lovely still:
Still for the sacred flock she spreads the fold,
For Sion rears the hill.

Mother she is, and cradle of our race,
A depth where treasures lie,
The broad foundation of a holy place,
Man's step to scale the sky.

She spreads the harvest-field which Angels reap,
  And lo ! the crop is white;
She spreads God's Acre where the happy sleep
  All night that is not night.

Earth may not pass till heaven shall pass away,
  Nor heaven may be renewed
Except with earth: and once more in that day
  Earth shall be very good.

THAT Eden of earth's sunrise cannot vie
  With Paradise beyond her sunset sky
    Hidden on high.

Four rivers watered Eden in her bliss,
But Paradise hath One which perfect is
    In sweetnesses.

Eden had gold, but Paradise hath gold
Like unto glass of splendours manifold
    Tongue hath not told.

Eden had sun and moon to make her bright;
But Paradise hath God and Lamb for light,
    And hath no night.

Unspotted innocence was Eden's best;
Great Paradise shows God's fulfilled behest,
    Triumph and rest.

Hail, Eve and Adam, source of death and shame!
New life has sprung from death, and Jesu's
    Name
    Clothes you with fame.

Hail Adam, and hail Eve! your children rise
And call you blessed, in their glad surmise
    Of Paradise.

QUINQUAGESIMA.

LOVE is alone the worthy law of love:
    All other laws have presupposed a taint:
  Love is the law from kindled saint to saint,
From lamb to lamb, from dove to answering dove.
Love is the motive of all things that move
    Harmonious by free will without constraint:
  Love learns and teaches: love shall man acquaint
With all he lacks, which all his lack is love.
Because Love is the fountain, I discern
    The stream as love: for what but love should
      flow
     From fountain Love? not bitter from the
      sweet!
  I ignorant, have I laid claim to know?
    Oh, teach me, Love, such knowledge as is meet
For one to know who is fain to love and learn.

PITEOUS my rhyme is
What while I muse of love and pain,
Of love misspent, of love in vain,
Of love that is not loved again:
   And is this all then?
   As long as time is,
Love loveth. Time is but a span,
The dalliance space of dying man:
And is this all immortals can?
   The gain were small then.

   Love loves for ever,
And finds a sort of joy in pain,
And gives with nought to take again,
And loves too well to end in vain:
   Is the gain small then?
   Love laughs at "never,"
Outlives our life, exceeds the span
Appointed to mere mortal man:
All which love is and does and can
   Is all in all then.

ASH WEDNESDAY.

MY God, my God, have mercy on my sin,
   For it is great; and if I should begin
To tell it all, the day would be too small
      To tell it in.

My God, Thou wilt have mercy on my sin
For Thy Love's sake: yea, if I should begin
To tell This all, the day would be too small
      To tell it in.

Some Feasts and Fasts.

GOOD Lord, to-day
   I scarce find breath to say:
  Scourge, but receive me.
For stripes are hard to bear, but worse
Thy intolerable curse;
  So do not leave me.

Good Lord, lean down
In pity, tho' Thou frown;
  Smite, but retrieve me:
For so Thou hold me up to stand
And kiss Thy smiting hand,
  It less will grieve me.

LENT.

IT is good to be last not first,
   Pending the present distress;
It is good to hunger and thirst,
  So it be for righteousness.
It is good to spend and be spent,
  It is good to watch and to pray:
Life and Death make a goodly Lent
  So it leads us to Easter Day.

E

EMBERTIDE.

SAW a Saint.—How canst thou tell that he
Thou sawest was a Saint?—
I saw one like to Christ so luminously
By patient deeds of love, his mortal taint
Seemed made his groundwork for humility.

And when he marked me downcast utterly
Where foul I sat and faint,
Then more than ever Christ-like kindled he;
And welcomed me as I had been a saint,
Tenderly stooping low to comfort me.

Christ bade him, "Do thou likewise." Wherefore he
Waxed zealous to acquaint
His soul with sin and sorrow, if so be
He might retrieve some latent saint:—
"Lo, I, with the child God hath given to me!"

MID-LENT.

IS any grieved or tired? Yea, by God's Will:
Surely God's Will alone is good and best:
O weary man, in weariness take rest,
O hungry man, by hunger feast thy fill.
Discern thy good beneath a mask of ill,
Or build of loneliness thy secret nest:
At noon take heart, being mindful of the west,
At night wake hope, for dawn advances still.

At night wake hope. Poor soul, in such sore need
  Of wakening and of girding up anew,
  Hast thou that hope which fainting doth pursue?
    No saint but hath pursued and hath been
      faint;
Bid love wake hope, for both thy steps shall speed,
  Still faint yet still pursuing, O thou saint.

PASSIONTIDE.

IT is the greatness of Thy love, dear Lord,
    that we would celebrate
  With sevenfold powers.
Our love at best is cold and poor, at best unseemly
    for Thy state,
  This best of ours.
Creatures that die, we yet are such as Thine own
    hands deigned to create:
  We frail as flowers,
We bitter bondslaves ransomed at a price incom-
    parably great
  To grace Heaven's bowers.

Thou callest: " Come at once "—and still Thou
    callest us: "Come late, tho' late"—
  (The moments fly)—
" Come, every one that thirsteth, come "—" Come
    prove Me, knocking at My gate"—
  (Some souls draw nigh!)—
" Come thou who waiting seekest Me"—" Come
    thou for whom I seek and wait"—
  (Why will we die?)—

"Come and repent: come and amend: come joy
  the joys unsatiate"—
 —(Christ passeth by . . .)—
 Lord, pass not by—I come—and I—and I.
 Amen.

✣

PALM SUNDAY.

**"He treadeth the winepress of the fierceness
and wrath of Almighty God."**

 LIFT mine eyes, and see
 Thee, tender Lord, in pain upon the tree,
Athirst for my sake and athirst for me.

"Yea, look upon Me there,
Compassed with thorns and bleeding everywhere,
For thy sake bearing all, and glad to bear."

I lift my heart to pray:
Thou Who didst love me all that darkened day,
Wilt Thou not love me to the end alway?

"Yea, thee My wandering sheep,
Yea, thee My scarlet sinner slow to weep,
Come to Me, I will love thee and will keep."

Yet am I racked with fear:
Behold the unending outer darkness drear,
Behold the gulf unbridgeable and near!

"Nay, fix thy heart, thine eyes,
Thy hope upon My boundless sacrifice:
Will I lose lightly one so dear-bought prize?"

Ah, Lord; it is not Thou,
Thou that wilt fail; yet woe is me, for how
Shall I endure who half am failing now?

"Nay, weld thy resolute will
To Mine: glance not aside for good or ill:
I love thee; trust Me still and love Me still."

Yet Thou Thyself hast said,
When Thou shalt sift the living from the dead
Some must depart shamed and uncomforted.

"Judge not before that day:
Trust Me with all thy heart, even tho' I slay:
Trust Me in love, trust on, love on, and pray.'

MONDAY IN HOLY WEEK.

"The Voice of my Beloved."

ONCE I ached for thy dear sake:
Wilt thou cause Me now to ache?
Once I bled for thee in pain:
Wilt thou rend My Heart again?
Crown of thorns and shameful tree,
Bitter death I bore for thee,
Bore My Cross to carry thee,
And wilt thou have nought of Me?

TUESDAY IN HOLY WEEK.

BY Thy long-drawn anguish to atone,
Jesus Christ, show mercy on Thine own:
Jesus Christ, show mercy and atone
Not for other sake except Thine own.

Thou Who thirsting on the Cross didst see
All mankind and all I love and me,
Still from Heaven look down in love and see
All mankind and all I love and me.

WEDNESDAY IN HOLY WEEK.

MAN'S life is death. Yet Christ endured
to live,
Preaching and teaching, toiling to and fro,
Few men accepting what He yearned to give,
Few men with eyes to know
His Face, that Face of Love He stooped to show.

Man's death is life. For Christ endured to die
In slow unuttered weariness of pain,
A curse and an astonishment, passed by,
Pointed at, mocked again
By men for whom He shed His Blood—in vain?

Some Feasts and Fasts.

MAUNDY THURSDAY.

*"And the Vine said . . . Should I leave my
wine, which cheereth God and man, and
go to be promoted over the trees?"*

THE great Vine left its glory to reign as Forest
    King.
"Nay," quoth the lofty forest trees, "we will not
    have this thing;
We will not have this supple one enring us with
    its ring.
Lo, from immemorial time our might towers
    shadowing:
Not we were born to curve and droop, not we
    to climb and cling:
We buffet back the buffeting wind, tough to its
    buffeting:
We screen great beasts, the wild fowl build in our
    heads and sing,
Every bird of every feather from off our tops takes
    wing:
I a king, and thou a king, and what king shall be
    our king?"

Nevertheless the great Vine stooped to be the
    Forest King,
While the forest swayed and murmured like seas
    that are tempesting:
Stooped and drooped with thousand tendrils in
    thirsty languishing;

Bowed to earth and lay on earth for earth's re-
    plenishing;
Put off sweetness, tasted bitterness, endured time's
    fashioning;
Put off life and put on death: and lo! it was all
    to bring
All its fellows down to a death which hath lost
    the sting,
All its fellows up to a life in endless triumphing,—
I a king, and thou a king, and this King to be
    our King.

GOOD FRIDAY MORNING.

"Bearing His Cross."

UP Thy Hill of Sorrows
    Thou all alone,
Jesus, man's Redeemer,
    Climbing to a Throne:
Thro' the world triumphant,
    Thro' the Church in pain,
Which think to look upon Thee
    No more again.

Upon my hill of sorrows
    I, Lord, with Thee,
Cheered, upheld, yea, carried,
    If a need should be:
Cheered, upheld, yea, carried,
    Never left alone,
Carried in Thy heart of hearts
    To a throne.

Some Feasts and Fasts.

GOOD FRIDAY.

LORD Jesus Christ, grown faint upon the Cross,
  A sorrow beyond sorrow in Thy look,
The unutterable craving for my soul;
    Thy love of me sufficed
To load upon Thee and make good my loss
  In face of darkened heaven and earth that
      shook :—
    In face of earth and heaven, take Thou my
        whole
      Heart, O Lord Jesus Christ.

GOOD FRIDAY EVENING.

"Bring forth the Spear."

NO Cherub's heart or hand for us might ache,
  No Seraph's heart of fire had half sufficed:
Thine own were pierced and broken for our sake,
    O Jesus Christ.

Therefore we love Thee with our faint good-will,
  We crave to love Thee not as heretofore,
To love Thee much, to love Thee more, and still
    More and yet more.

"A bundle of myrrh is my Well=beloved unto me."

THY Cross cruciferous doth flower in all
  And every cross, dear Lord, assigned to us:
Ours lowly-statured crosses; Thine how tall,
  Thy Cross cruciferous.

Thy Cross alone life-giving, glorious:
For love of Thine, souls love their own when small,
  Easy and light, or great and ponderous.

Since deep calls deep, Lord, hearken when we call;
  When cross calls Cross racking and emulous:—
Remember us with him who shared Thy gall,
  Thy Cross cruciferous.

EASTER EVEN.

THE tempest over and gone, the calm begun,
  Lo, "it is finished" and the Strong Man
    sleeps:
All stars keep vigil watching for the sun,
  The moon her vigil keeps.

A garden full of silence and of dew
  Beside a virgin cave and entrance stone:
Surely a garden full of Angels too,
  Wondering, on watch, alone.

Some Feasts and Fasts.

They who cry "Holy, Holy, Holy," still
   Veiling their faces round God's Throne above,
May well keep vigil on this heavenly hill
   And cry their cry of love,

Adoring God in His new mystery
   Of Love more deep than hell, more strong
     than death;
Until the day break and the shadows flee,
   The Shaking and the Breath.

Our Church Palms are budding willow twigs.

WHILE Christ lay dead the widowed world
   Wore willow green for hope undone:
Till, when bright Easter dews impearled
   The chilly burial earth,
All north and south, all east and west,
   Flushed rosy in the arising sun;
Hope laughed, and Faith resumed her rest,
   And Love remembered mirth.

EASTER DAY.

WORDS cannot utter
   Christ His returning:
Mankind, keep jubilee,
   Strip off your mourning,
Crown you with garlands,
   Set your lamps burning.

Speech is left speechless;
 Set you to singing,
Fling your hearts open wide,
 Set your bells ringing:
Christ the Chief Reaper
 Comes, His sheaf bringing.

Earth wakes her song-birds,
 Puts on her flowers,
Leads out her lambkins,
 Builds up her bowers:
This is man's spousal day,
 Christ's day and ours.

EASTER MONDAY.

OUT in the rain a world is growing green,
 On half the trees quick buds are seen
Where glued-up buds have been.
Out in the rain God's Acre stretches green,
 Its harvest quick tho' still unseen:
 For there the Life hath been.

If Christ hath died His brethren well may die,
 Sing in the gate of death, lay by
 This life without a sigh:
For Christ hath died and good it is to die;
 To sleep whenso He lays us by,
 Then wake without a sigh.

Yea, Christ hath died, yea, Christ is risen again:
  Wherefore both life and death grow plain
    To us who wax and wane;
For Christ Who rose shall die no more again:
  Amen: till He makes all things plain
    Let us wax on and wane.

EASTER TUESDAY.

" TOGETHER with my dead body shall they
    arise."
Shall my dead body arise? then amen and yea
On track of a home beyond the uttermost skies
  Together with my dead body shall they.

We know the way: thank God Who hath showed
        us the way!
Jesus Christ our Way to beautiful Paradise,
Jesus Christ the Same for ever, the Same to-day.

Five Virgins replenish with oil their lamps, being
      wise,
  Five Virgins awaiting the Bridegroom watch
      and pray:
And if I one day spring from my grave to the
      prize,
  Together with my dead body shall they.

Some Feasts and Fasts.

ROGATIONTIDE.

WHO scatters tares shall reap no wheat,
But go hungry while others eat.

Who sows the wind shall not reap grain;
The sown wind whirleth back again.

What God opens must open be,
Tho' man pile the sand of the sea.

What God shuts is opened no more,
Tho' man weary himself to find the door.

ASCENSION EVE.

LORD Almighty, Who hast formed us weak,
    With us whom Thou hast formed deal
        fatherly;
Be found of us whom Thou hast deigned to seek,
    Be found that we the more may seek for Thee;
Lord, speak and grant us ears to hear Thee speak;
    Lord, come to us and grant us eyes to see;
Lord, make us meek, for Thou Thyself art meek;
    Lord, Thou art Love, fill us with charity.
O Thou the Life of living and of dead,
    Who givest more the more Thyself hast given,
        Suffice us as Thy saints Thou hast sufficed;
That beautified, replenished, comforted,
    Still gazing off from earth and up at heaven
        We may pursue Thy steps, Lord Jesus Christ.

ASCENSION DAY.

"A Cloud received Him out of their sight."

WHEN Christ went up to Heaven the Apostles
    stayed
Gazing at Heaven with souls and wills on fire,
Their hearts on flight along the track He made,
    Winged by desire.

Their silence spake : " Lord, why not follow Thee ?
    Home is not home without Thy Blessed Face,
Life is not life. Remember, Lord, and see,
    Look back, embrace.

"Earth is one desert waste of banishment,
    Life is one long-drawn anguish of decay.
Where Thou wert wont to go we also went :
    Why not to-day ? "

Nevertheless a cloud cut off their gaze :
    They tarry to build up Jerusalem,
Watching for Him, while thro' the appointed days
    He watches them.

They do His Will, and doing it rejoice,
    Patiently glad to spend and to be spent :
Still He speaks to them, still they hear His Voice
    And are content.

For as a cloud received Him from their sight,
    So with a cloud will He return ere long :
Therefore they stand on guard by day, by night,
    Strenuous and strong.

They do, they dare, they beyond seven times seven
    Forgive, they cry God's mighty word aloud:
Yet sometimes haply lift tired eyes to Heaven —
    "Is that His cloud?"

WHITSUN EVE.

"AS many as I love."—Ah, Lord, Who lovest all,
If thus it is with Thee why sit remote above,
Beholding from afar, stumbling and marred and
    small,
    So many Thou dost love?

Whom sin and sorrow make their worn reluctant
    thrall;
    Who fain would flee away but lack the wings
        of dove;
Who long for love and rest; who look to Thee,
    and call
    To Thee for rest and love.

WHITSUN DAY.

"When the Day of Pentecost was fully come."

AT sound as of rushing wind, and sight as of
        fire,
    Lo! flesh and blood made spirit and fiery flame,
    Ambassadors in Christ's and the Father's Name,
        To woo back a world's desire.

These men chose death for their life and shame
for their boast,
For fear courage, for doubt intuition of faith,
Chose love that is strong as death and stronger
than death
In the power of the Holy Ghost.

WHITSUN MONDAY.

"A pure River of Water of Life."

WE know not a voice of that River,
If vocal or silent it be,
Where for ever and ever and ever
It flows to no sea.

More deep than the seas is that River,
More full than their manifold tides,
Where for ever and ever and ever
It flows and abides.

Pure gold is the bed of that River
(The gold of that land is the best),
Where for ever and ever and ever
It flows on at rest.

Oh goodly the banks of that River,
Oh goodly the fruits that they bear,
Where for ever and ever and ever
It flows and is fair.

For lo! on each bank of that River
The Tree of Life life-giving grows,
Where for ever and ever and ever
The Pure River flows.

F

WHITSUN TUESDAY.

LORD Jesus Christ, our Wisdom and our Rest,
    Who wisely dost reveal and wisely hide,
  Grant us such grace in wisdom to abide
According to Thy Will whose Will is best.
Contented with Thine uttermost behest,
    Too sweet for envy and too high for pride ;
  All simple-souled, dove-hearted and dove-eyed,
Soft-voiced, and satisfied in humble nest.
Wondering at the bounty of Thy Love
    Which gives us wings of silver and of gold ;
    Wings folded close, yet ready to unfold
      When Thou shalt say, " Winter is past and
        gone : "
When Thou shalt say, " Spouse, sister, love and
      dove,
    Come hither, sit with Me upon My Throne."

TRINITY SUNDAY.

MY God, Thyself being Love Thy heart is love,
    And love Thy Will and love Thy Word
        to us,
  Whether Thou show us depths calamitous
Or heights and flights of rapturous peace above.
O Christ the Lamb, O Holy Ghost the Dove,
    Reveal the Almighty Father unto us ;
    That we may tread Thy courts felicitous,
Loving Who loves us, for our God is Love.

Lo, if our God be Love thro' heaven's long day,
   Love is He thro' our mortal pilgrimage,
     Love was He thro' all aeons that are told.
We change, but Thou remainest; for Thine
     age
     Is, Was, and Is to come, nor new nor old;
We change, but Thou remainest; yea and yea!

CONVERSION OF ST. PAUL.

 BLESSED Paul elect to grace,
     Arise and wash away thy sin,
Anoint thy head and wash thy face,
     Thy gracious course begin.
To start thee on thy outrunning race
Christ shows the splendour of His Face:
What will that Face of splendour be
When at the goal He welcomes thee?

IN weariness and painfulness St. Paul
     Served God and pleased Him: after-saints
        no less
Can wait on and can please Him, one and all
     In weariness and painfulness,

By faith and hope triumphant thro' distress:
Not with the rankling service of a thrall;
     But even as loving children trust and bless.

F 2

Weep and rejoice, answering their Father's call,
  Work with tired hands, and forward upward
      press
On sore tired feet still rising when they fall,
  In weariness and painfulness.

VIGIL OF THE PRESENTATION.

LONG and dark the nights, dim and short
    the days,
Mounting weary heights on our weary ways,
  Thee our God we praise.
Scaling heavenly heights by unearthly ways,
Thee our God we praise all our nights and days,
  Thee our God we praise.

FEAST OF THE PRESENTATION.

FIRSTFRUITS of our grain,
  Infant and Lamb appointed to be slain,
A Virgin and two doves were all Thy train,
With one old man for state,
When Thou didst enter first Thy Father's gate.

Since then Thy train hath been
Freeman and bondman, bishop, king and queen,
With flaming candles and with garlands green:
Oh happy all who wait
One day or thousand days around Thy gate.

And these have offered Thee,
Beside their hearts, great stores for charity,
Gold, frankincense and myrrh; if such may be
For savour or for state
Within the threshold of Thy golden gate.

Then snowdrops and my heart
I'll bring, to find those blacker than Thou art:
Yet, loving Lord, accept us in good part;
And give me grace to wait
A bruised reed bowed low before Thy gate.

THE PURIFICATION OF ST. MARY
THE VIRGIN.

PURITY born of a Maid:
Was such a Virgin defiled?
Nay, by no shade of a shade.
She offered her gift of pure love,
A dove with a fair fellow-dove.
She offered her Innocent Child
The Essence and Author of Love;
The Lamb that indwelt by the Dove
Was spotless and holy and mild;
More pure than all other,
More pure than His Mother,
Her God and Redeemer and Child.

VIGIL OF THE ANNUNCIATION.

ALL weareth, all wasteth,
All flitteth, all hasteth,
All of flesh and time :—
Sound, sweet heavenly chime,
Ring in the unutterable eternal prime.

Man hopeth, man feareth,
Man droopeth :—Christ cheereth,
Compassing release,
Comforting with peace,
Promising rest where strife and anguish cease.

Saints waking, saints sleeping,
Rest well in safe keeping;
Well they rest to-day
While they watch and pray,—
But their to-morrow's rest what tongue shall say?

FEAST OF THE ANNUNCIATION.

WHERETO shall we liken this Blessed Mary
Virgin,
Fruitful shoot from Jesse's root graciously emerg-
ing?
Lily we might call her, but Christ alone is white;
Rose delicious, but that Jesus is the one Delight;
Flower of women, but her Firstborn is mankind's
one flower:
He the Sun lights up all moons thro' their radiant
hour.

"Blessed among women, highly favoured," thus
Glorious Gabriel hailed her, teaching words to us:
Whom devoutly copying we too cry "All hail!"
Echoing on the music of glorious Gabriel.

HERSELF a rose, who bore the Rose,
   She bore the Rose and felt its thorn.
All Loveliness new-born
Took on her bosom its repose,
   And slept and woke there night and morn.

Lily herself, she bore the one
   Fair Lily; sweeter, whiter, far
   Than she or others are:
The Sun of Righteousness her Son,
   She was His morning star.

She gracious, He essential Grace,
   He was the Fountain, she the rill:
   Her goodness to fulfil
And gladness, with proportioned pace
   He led her steps thro' good and ill.

Christ's mirror she of grace and love,
   Of beauty and of life and death:
   By hope and love and faith
Transfigured to His Likeness, "Dove,
   Spouse, Sister, Mother," Jesus saith.

Some Feasts and Fasts.

ST. MARK.

ONCE like a broken bow Mark sprang
    aside :
Yet grace recalled him to a worthier course,
To feeble hands and knees increasing force,
    Till God was magnified.

And now a strong Evangelist, St. Mark
Hath for his sign a Lion in his strength;
And thro' the stormy water's breadth and
    length
    He helps to steer God's Ark.

Thus calls he sinners to be penitents,
He kindles penitents to high desire,
He mounts before them to the sphere of saints,
    And bids them come up higher.

ST. BARNABAS.

"Now when we had discovered Cyprus, we
left it on the left hand."—*Acts* xxi. 3.
"We sailed under Cyprus, because the winds
were contrary."—*Acts* xxvii. 4.

ST. Barnabas, with John his sister's son,
    Set sail for Cyprus; leaving in their wake
  That chosen Vessel, who for Jesus' sake
Proclaimed the Gentiles and the Jews at one.
Divided while united, each must run
    His mighty course not hell should overtake;
  And pressing toward the mark must own the ache
Of love, and sigh for heaven not yet begun.

For saints in life-long exile yearn to touch
  Warm human hands, and commune face to face ;
    But these we know not ever met again:
Yet once St. Paul at distance overmuch
    Just sighted Cyprus; and once more in vain
Neared it and passed ;—not there his landing-
     place.

✤

VIGIL OF ST. PETER.

 JESU, gone so far apart
    Only my heart can follow Thee,
That look which pierced St. Peter's heart
    Turn now on me.

Thou who dost search me thro' and thro'
    And mark the crooked ways I went,
Look on me, Lord, and make me too
    Thy penitent.

✤

ST. PETER.

" LAUNCH out into the deep," Christ spake
    of old
  To Peter: and he launched into the deep;
  Strengthened should tempest wake which lay
     asleep,
Strengthened to suffer heat or suffer cold.
Thus, in Christ's Prescience: patient to behold
  A fall, a rise, a scaling Heaven's high steep;
  Prescience of Love, which deigned to overleap
The mire of human errors manifold.

Lord, Lover of Thy Peter, and of him
  Beloved with craving of a humbled heart
    Which eighteen hundred years have satisfied;
Hath he his throne among Thy Seraphim
  Who love? or sits he on a throne apart,
    Unique, near Thee, to love Thee human-eyed?

ST. Peter once: "Lord, dost Thou wash my
  feet?"—
Much more I say: Lord, dost Thou stand and
  knock
At my closed heart more rugged than a rock,
Bolted and barred, for Thy soft touch unmeet,
Nor garnished nor in any wise made sweet?
  Owls roost within and dancing satyrs mock.
  Lord, I have heard the crowing of the cock
And have not wept: ah, Lord, Thou knowest it.
Yet still I hear Thee knocking, still I hear:
  "Open to Me, look on Me eye to eye,
    That I may wring thy heart and make it whole;
And teach thee love because I hold thee dear,
    And sup with thee in gladness soul with soul,
  And sup with thee in glory by and by."

I FOLLOWED Thee, my God, I followed Thee
  To see the end:
I turned back flying from Gethsemane,
Turned back on flying steps to see
  Thy Face, my God, my Friend.

Even fleeing from Thee my heart clave to Thee:
  I turned perforce
Constrained, yea chained by love which maketh
      free;
I turned perforce, and silently
  Followed along Thy course.

Lord, didst Thou know that I was following
      Thee?
  I weak and small
Yet Thy true lover, mean tho' I must be,
Sinning and sorrowing—didst Thou see?
  O Lord, Thou sawest all.

I thought I had been strong to die for Thee;
  I disbelieved
Thy word of warning spoken patiently:
My heart cried, "That be far from me,"
  Till Thy bruised heart I grieved.

Once I had urged: "Lord, this be far from
      Thee:"—-
  Rebel to light,
It needed first that Thou shouldst die for me
Or ever I could plumb and see
  Love's lovely depth and height.

Alas that I should trust myself, not Thee;
  Not trust Thy word:
I faithless slumberer in Gethsemane,
Blinded and rash; who instantly
  Put trust, but in a sword.

Ah Lord, if even at the last in Thee
   I had put faith,
I might even at the last have counselled me,
And not have heaped up cruelty
   To sting Thee in Thy death.

Alas for me, who bore to think on Thee
   And yet to lie:
While Thou, O Lord, didst bear to look on me
Goaded by fear to blasphemy,
   And break my heart and die.

No balm I find in Gilead, yet in Thee
   Nailed to Thy palm
I find a balm that wrings and comforts me:
Balm wrung from Thee by agony,
   My balm, mine only balm.

Oh blessed John who standeth close to Thee,
   With Magdalene,
And Thine own Mother praying silently,
Yea, blessed above women she,
   Now blessed even as then.

And blessed the scorned thief who hangs by Thee,
   Whose thirsting mouth
Thirsts for Thee more than water, whose eyes see,
Whose lips confess in ecstasy
   Nor feel their parching drouth.

Like as the hart the water-brooks I Thee
   Desire, my hands
I stretch to Thee; O kind Lord, pity me:
Lord, I have wept, wept bitterly,
   I driest of dry lands.

Lord, I am standing far far off from Thee;
　　Yet is my heart
Hanging with Thee upon the accursed tree;
The nails, the thorns, pierce Thee and me:
　　My God, I claim my part

Scarce in Thy throne and kingdom; yet with
　　Thee
　　In shame, in loss,
In Thy forsaking, in Thine agony:
Love crucified, behold even me,
　　Me also bear Thy cross.

VIGIL OF ST. BARTHOLOMEW.

LORD, to Thine own grant watchful hearts
　　and eyes;
　　Hearts strung to prayer, awake while eyelids
　　　sleep;
　　Eyes patient till the end to watch and weep.
So will sleep nourish power to wake and rise
With Virgins who keep vigil and are wise,
　　To sow among all sowers who shall reap,
　　From out man's deep to call Thy vaster deep,
And tread the uphill track to Paradise.
Sweet souls! so patient that they make no moan,
　　So calm on journey that they seem at rest,
　　　So rapt in prayer that half they dwell in
　　　　heaven
　　　Thankful for all withheld and all things given;
　　So lit by love that Christ shines manifest
Transfiguring their aspects to His own.

Some Feasts and Fasts.

ST. BARTHOLOMEW.

HE bore an agony whereof the name
    Hath turned his fellows pale:
But what if God should call us to the same,
    Should call, and we should fail?

Nor earth nor sea could swallow up our shame,
    Nor darkness draw a veil:
For he endured that agony whose name
    Hath made his fellows quail.

ST. MICHAEL AND ALL ANGELS.

"Ye that excel in strength."

SERVICE and strength, God's Angels and
    Archangels;
His Seraphs fires, and lamps His Cherubim:
Glory to God from highest and from lowest,
    Glory to God in everlasting hymn
      From all His creatures.

Princes that serve, and Powers that work His
    pleasure,
    Heights that soar to'ard Him, Depths that sink
      to'ard Him;
Flames fire out-flaming, chill beside His Essence;
    Insight all-probing, save where scant and dim
      To'ard its Creator.

Some Feasts and Fasts.

Sacred and free exultant in God's pleasure,
  His Will their solace, thus they wait on Him;
And shout their shout of ecstasy eternal,
  And trim their splendours that they burn not dim
    To'ard their Creator.

Wherefore with Angels, wherefore with Archangels,
  With lofty Cherubs, loftier Seraphim,
We laud and magnify our God Almighty,
  And veil our faces rendering love to Him
    With all His creatures.

VIGIL OF ALL SAINTS.

UP, my drowsing eyes!
    Up, my sinking heart!
Up to Jesus Christ arise!
  Claim your part
In all raptures of the skies.

Yet a little while,
  Yet a little way,
Saints shall reap and rest and smile
  All the day.
Up! let's trudge another mile.

ALL SAINTS.

AS grains of sand, as stars, as drops of dew,
  Numbered and treasured by the Almighty
    Hand,
  The Saints triumphant throng that holy land
Where all things and Jerusalem are new.

We know not half they sing or half they do,
  But this we know, they rest and understand;
  While like a conflagration freshly fanned
Their love glows upward, outward, thro' and thro'.
Lo! like a stream of incense launched on flame
  Fresh Saints stream up from death to life
    above,
  To shine among those others and rejoice:
What matters tribulation whence they came?
  All love and only love can find a voice
Where God makes glad His Saints, for God is
    Love.

ALL SAINTS: MARTYRS.

ONCE slain for Him who first was slain for
    them,
  Now made alive in Him for evermore,
  All luminous and lovely in their gore
With no more buffeting winds or tides to stem
The Martyrs look for New Jerusalem;
  And cry "How long?" remembering all they
    bore,
  "How long?" with heart and eyes sent on
    before
Toward consummated throne and diadem.
  "How long?" White robes are given to their
    desire;
  "How long?" deep rest that is and is to be;
    With a great promise of the oncoming host,
Loves to their love and fires to flank their fire:
  So rest they, worshipping incessantly
    One God, the Father, Son, and Holy Ghost.

"I gave a sweet smell."

SAINTS are like roses when they flush rarest,
  Saints are like lilies when they bloom fairest,
    Saints are like violets sweetest of their kind:
        Bear in mind
      This to-day. Then to-morrow:
All like roses rarer than the rarest,
All like lilies fairer than the fairest,
    All like violets sweeter than we know.
        Be it so.
      To-morrow blots out sorrow.

HARK! the Alleluias of the great salvation
  Still beginning, never ending, still begin,
The thunder of an endless adoration:
Open ye the gates, that the righteous nation
  Which have kept the truth may enter in.

Roll ye back, ye pearls, on your twelvefold station:
  No more deaths to die, no more fights to win!
Lift your heads, ye gates, that the righteous nation
Led by the Great Captain of their sole salvation,
  Having kept the truth, may enter in.

G

A SONG FOR THE LEAST OF ALL SAINTS.

LOVE is the key of life and death,
  Of hidden heavenly mystery:
Of all Christ is, of all He saith,
  Love is the key.

As three times to His Saint He saith,
  He saith to me, He saith to thee,
Breathing His Grace-conferring Breath:
  "Lovest thou Me?"

Ah, Lord, I have such feeble faith,
  Such feeble hope to comfort me:
But love it is, is strong as death,
  And I love Thee.

SUNDAY BEFORE ADVENT.

THE end of all things is at hand. We all
  Stand in the balance trembling as we stand;
Or if not trembling, tottering to a fall.
  The end of all things is at hand.

O hearts of men, covet the unending land!
O hearts of men, covet the musical,
  Sweet, never-ending waters of that strand!

While Earth shows poor, a slippery rolling ball,
  And Hell looms vast, a gulf unplumbed, un-
    spanned,
And Heaven flings wide its gates to great and
    small,
  The end of all things is at hand.

�֍

GIFTS AND GRACES.

✤

GIFTS AND GRACES.

LOVE loveth Thee, and wisdom loveth Thee:
    The love that loveth Thee sits satisfied;
  Wisdom that loveth Thee grows million-eyed,
Learning what was, and is, and is to be.
Wisdom and love are glad of all they see;
    Their heart is deep, their hope is not denied;
    They rock at rest on time's unresting tide,
And wait to rest thro' long eternity.
Wisdom and love and rest, each holy soul
    Hath these to-day while day is only night:
    What shall souls have when morning brings to
        light
        Love, wisdom, rest, God's treasure stored
        above?
Palm shall they have, and harp and aureole,
        Wisdom, rest, love—and lo! the whole is
        love.

LORD, give me love that I may love Thee
    much,
  Yea, give me love that I may love Thee more,
  And all for love may worship and adore
And touch Thee with love's consecrated touch.

I halt to-day; be love my cheerful crutch,
  My feet to plod, some day my wings to soar:
  Some day; but, Lord, not any day before
Thou call me perfect, having made me such.
This is a day of love, a day of sorrow,
  Love tempering sorrow to a sort of bliss;
    A day that shortens while we call it long:
A longer day of love will dawn to-morrow,
  A longer, brighter, lovelier day than this,
    Endless, all love, no sorrow, but a song.

"Tis a king, ... unto the King."

LOVE doth so grace and dignify
  That beggars treat as king with king
Before the Throne of God most High:
Love recognises love's own cry,
  And stoops to take love's offering.

A loving heart, tho' soiled and bruised;
  A kindling heart, tho' cold before;
Who ever came and was refused
By Love? Do, Lord, as Thou art used
  To do, and make me love Thee more.

YE who love to-day,
  Turn away
From Patience with her silver ray:
  For Patience shows a twilight face,
    Like a half-lighted moon
  When daylight dies apace.

But ye who love to-morrow
Beg or borrow
To-day some bitterness of sorrow:
  For Patience shows a lustrous face,
    In depth of night her noon;
  Then to her sun gives place.

IFE that was born to-day
  Must make no stay,
    But tend to end
As blossom-bloom of May.
O Lord, confirm my root,
Train up my shoot,
    To live and give
Harvest of wholesome fruit.

Life that was born to die
Sets heart on high,
    And counts and mounts
Steep stages of the sky.
Two things, Lord, I desire
And I require ;
    Love's name, and flame
To wrap my soul in fire.

Life that was born to love
Sends heart above
    Both cloud and shroud,
And broods a peaceful dove.
Two things I ask of Thee ;
Deny not me ;
    Eyesight and light
Thy Blessed Face to see.

"Perfect Love casteth out Fear."

LORD, give me blessed fear,
　　And much more blessed love
That fearing I may love Thee here
　　And be Thy harmless dove:

Until Thou cast out fear,
　　Until Thou perfect love,
Until Thou end mine exile here
　　And fetch Thee home Thy dove.

HOPE is the counterpoise of fear
　　While night enthralls us here.

Fear hath a startled eye that holds a tear:
Hope hath an upward glance, for dawn draws
　　　near
With sunshine and with cheer.
Fear gazing earthwards spies a bier;
And sets herself to rear
A lamentable tomb where leaves drop sere,
Bleaching to congruous skeletons austere:
Hope chants a funeral hymn most sweet and clear,
And seems true chanticleer
Of resurrection and of all things dear
In the oncoming endless year.

Fear ballasts hope, hope buoys up fear,
And both befit us here.

"Subject to like Passions as we are."

WHOSO hath anguish is not dead in sin,
   Whoso hath pangs of utterless desire.
Like as in smouldering flax which harbours
    fire,—
Red heat of conflagration may begin,
Melt that hard heart, burn out the dross within,
   Permeate with glory the new man entire,
   Crown him with fire, mould for his hands a
    lyre
Of fiery strings to sound with those who win.
Anguish is anguish, yet potential bliss,
   Pangs of desire are birth-throes of delight;
   Those citizens felt such who walk in white,
And meet, but no more sunder, with a kiss;
Who fathom still unfathomed mysteries,
   And love, adore, rejoice, with all their might.

EXPERIENCE bows a sweet contented face,
   Still setting to her seal that God is true:
   Beneath the sun, she knows, is nothing new;
All things that go return with measured pace,
Winds, rivers, man's still recommencing race:—
   While Hope beyond earth's circle strains her
    view,
   Past sun and moon, and rain and rainbow too,
Enamoured of unseen eternal grace.

Experience saith, "My God doth all things well:"
And for the morrow taketh little care,
    Such peace and patience garrison her soul:—
    While Hope, who never yet hath eyed the goal,
With arms flung forth, and backward floating hair,
Touches, embraces, hugs the invisible.

"Charity never Faileth."

SUCH is Love, it comforts in extremity,
    Tho' a tempest rage around and rage above,
Tempest beyond tempest, far as eye can see:
    Such is Love,

That it simply heeds its mourning inward Dove;
Dove which craves contented for a home to be
    Set amid the myrtles or an olive grove.

Dove-eyed Love contemplates the Twelve-fruited
    Tree,
    Marks the bowing palms which worship as they
      move;
Simply sayeth, simply prayeth, "All for me!"
    Such is Love.

"The Greatest of these is Charity."

A MOON impoverished amid stars curtailed,
    A sun of its exuberant lustre shorn,
    A transient morning that is scarcely morn,
A lingering night in double dimness veiled.—

Our hands are slackened and our strength has
    failed:
  We born to darkness, wherefore were we born?
  No ripening more for olive, grape, or corn:
Faith faints, hope faints, even love himself has paled.
Nay! love lifts up a face like any rose
  Flushing and sweet above a thorny stem,
Softly protesting that the way he knows;
  And as for faith and hope, will carry them
  Safe to the gate of New Jerusalem,
Where light shines full and where the palm-tree
    blows.

ALL beneath the sun hasteth,
  All that hath begun wasteth;
Earth-notes change in tune
With the changeful moon,
Which waneth
While earth's chant complaineth.

Plumbs the deep, Fear descending;
Scales the steep, Hope ascending;
Faith betwixt the twain
Plies both goad and rein,
Half fearing,
All hopeful, day is nearing.

IF thou be dead, forgive and thou shalt live;
  If thou hast sinned, forgive and be forgiven;
God waiteth to be gracious and forgive,
    And open heaven.

Set not thy will to die and not to live;
  Set not thy face as flint refusing heaven;
Thou fool, set not thy heart on hell: forgive
    And be forgiven.

"Let Patience have her perfect work."

AN man rejoice who lives in hourly fear?
  Can man make haste who toils beneath a
    load?
Can man feel rest who has no fixed abode?
All he lays hold of, or can see or hear,
Is passing by, is prompt to disappear,
  Is doomed, foredoomed, continueth in no stay:
  This day he breathes in is his latter day,
This year of time is this world's latter year.
Thus in himself is he most miserable:
  Out of himself, Lord, lift him up to Thee,
  Out of himself and all these worlds that flee;
    Hold him in patience underneath the rod,
Anchor his hope beyond life's ebb and swell,
    Perfect his patience in the love of God.

ATIENCE must dwell with Love, for Love and
  Sorrow
Have pitched their tent together here:
Love all alone will build a house to-morrow,
  And sorrow not be near.

To-day for Love's sake hope, still hope, in sorrow,
  Rest in her shade and hold her dear:
To-day she nurses thee; and lo! to-morrow
  Love only will be near.

"Let everything that hath breath praise the Lord."

ALL that we see rejoices in the sunshine,
  All that we hear makes merry in the Spring:
God grant us such a mind to be glad after our kind,
    And to sing
His praises evermore for everything.

Much that we see must vanish with the sunshine,
  Sweet Spring must fail, and fail the choir of
     Spring:
But Wisdom shall burn on when the lesser lights
    are gone,
    And shall sing
God's praises evermore for everything.

WHAT is the beginning? Love. What the
  course? Love still.
What the goal? The goal is Love on the happy hill.
Is there nothing then but Love, search we sky or
  earth?
There is nothing out of Love hath perpetual worth:
All things flag but only Love, all things fail or flee;
There is nothing left but Love worthy you and me.

LORD, make me pure:
  Only the pure shall see Thee as Thou art
  And shall endure.
  Lord, bring me low;
For Thou wert lowly in Thy blessed heart:
  Lord, keep me so.

LOVE, to be love, must walk Thy way
    And work Thy Will;
      Or if Thou say, "Lie still,"
Lie still and pray.

Love, Thine own Bride, with all her might
    Will follow Thee,
      And till the shadows flee
Keep Thee in sight.

Love will not mar her peaceful face
    With cares undue,
      Faithless and hopeless too
And out of place.

Love, knowing Thou much more art Love.
    Will sun her grief,
      And pluck her myrtle-leaf,
And be Thy dove.

Love here hath vast beatitude:
    What shall be hers
      Where there is no more curse,
But all is good?

LORD, I am feeble and of mean account:
　　Thou Who dost condescend as well as
　　　　mount,
　　Stoop Thou Thyself to me
　　And grant me grace to hear and grace to see.

Lord, if Thou grant me grace to hear and see
Thy very Self Who stoopest thus to me,
　　I make but slight account
　　Of aught beside wherein to sink or mount.

TUNE me, O Lord, into one harmony
　　With Thee, one full responsive vibrant
　　　　chord;
Unto Thy praise all love and melody,
　　Tune me, O Lord.

　　Thus need I flee nor death, nor fire, nor
　　　　sword:
A little while these be, then cease to be,
　　And sent by Thee not these should be abhorred.

Devil and world, gird me with strength to flee,
　　To flee the flesh, and arm me with Thy word:
As Thy Heart is to my heart, unto Thee
　　Tune me, O Lord.

"They shall be as white as snow."

WHITENESS most white. Ah, to be clean again
In mine own sight and God's most holy sight!
To reach thro' any flood or fire of pain
   Whiteness most white:

To learn to hate the wrong and love the right
Even while I walk thro' shadows that are vain,
   Descending thro' vain shadows into night.

Lord, not to-day: yet some day bliss for bane
   Give me, for mortal frailty give me might,
Give innocence for guilt, and for my stain
   Whiteness most white.

THY lilies drink the dew,
   Thy lambs the rill, and I will drink them too;
   For those in purity
And innocence are types, dear Lord, of Thee.
   The fragrant lily flower
Bows and fulfils Thy Will its lifelong hour;
   The lamb at rest and play
Fulfils Thy Will in gladness all the day;
   They leave to-morrow's cares
Until the morrow, what it brings it bears.
   And I, Lord, would be such;
Not high or great or anxious overmuch

But pure and temperate,
Earnest to do Thy Will betimes and late,
  Fragrant with love and praise
And innocence thro' all my appointed days;
  Thy lily I would be,
Spotless and sweet, Thy lamb to follow Thee.

"When I was in trouble I called upon the Lord."

 BURDENED heart that bleeds and bears
    And hopes and waits in pain,
And faints beneath its fears and cares,
    Yet hopes again:

Wilt Thou accept the heart I bring,
    O gracious Lord and kind,
To ease it of a torturing sting,
    And staunch and bind?

Alas, if Thou wilt none of this,
    None else have I to give:
Look Thou upon it as it is,
    Accept, relieve.

Or if Thou wilt not yet relieve,
    Be not extreme to sift:
Accept a faltering will to give,
    Itself Thy gift.

H

Gifts and Graces.

CRANT us such grace that we may work
    Thy Will
And speak Thy words and walk before Thy Face,
Profound and calm, like waters deep and still:
    Grant us such grace.

Not hastening and not loitering in our pace
For gloomiest valley or for sultriest hill,
    Content and fearless on our downward race.

As rivers seek a sea they cannot fill
    But are themselves filled full in its embrace,
Absorbed, at rest, each river and each rill:
    Grant us such grace.

"Who hath despised the day of small things?"

AS violets so be I recluse and sweet,
    Cheerful as daisies unaccounted rare,
Still sunward-gazing from a lowly seat,
    Still sweetening wintry air.

While half-awakened Spring lags incomplete,
    While lofty forest trees tower bleak and bare,
Daisies and violets own remotest heat
    And bloom and make them fair.

"Do this, and he doeth it."

CONTENT to come, content to go,
   Content to wrestle or to race,
Content to know or not to know,
    Each in his place;

Lord, grant us grace to love Thee so
   That glad of heart and glad of face
At last we may sit, high or low,
    Each in his place;

Where pleasures flow as rivers flow,
   And loss has left no barren trace,
And all that are, are perfect so,
    Each in his place.

"That no man take thy Crown."

BE faithful unto death. Christ proffers thee
   Crown of a life that draws immortal breath:
To thee He saith, yea, and He saith to me,
   "Be faithful unto death."

To every living soul that same He saith,
  "Be faithful":—whatsoever else we be,
   Let us be faithful, challenging His faith.

Tho' trouble storm around us like the sea,
   Tho' hell surge up to scare us and to scathe,
Tho' heaven and earth betake themselves to flee,
  "Be faithful unto death."

H 2

"Ye are come unto Mount Sion."

FEAR, Faith, and Hope have sent their hearts
    above:
Prudence, Obedience, and Humility
Climb at their call, all scaling heaven toward
    Love.
Fear hath least grace but great expediency;
    Faith and Humility show grave and strong;
    Prudence and Hope mount balanced equally.
Obedience marches marshalling their throng,
    Goes first, goes last, to left hand or to right;
    And all the six uplift a pilgrim's song.
By day they rest not, nor they rest by night:
    While Love within them, with them, over them,
    Weans them and woos them from the dark to
      light.
Each plies for staff not reed with broken stem,
    But olive branch in pledge of patient peace;
    Till Love being theirs in New Jerusalem,
Transfigure them to Love, and so they cease.
    Love is the sole beatitude above:
    All other graces, to their vast increase
Of glory, look on Love and mirror Love.

"Sit down in the lowest room."

LORD, give me grace
    To take the lowest place;
Nor even desire,
Unless it be Thy Will, to go up higher.

Gifts and Graces.

Except by grace,
I fail of lowest place;
Except desire
Sit low, it aims awry to go up higher.

"Lord, it is good for us to be here."

GRANT us, O Lord, that patience and that
    faith:
Faith's patience imperturbable in Thee,
Hope's patience till the long-drawn shadows flee,
Love's patience unresentful of all scathe.
Verily we need patience breath by breath;
    Patience while faith holds up her glass to see,
    While hope toils yoked in fear's copartnery,
And love goes softly on the way to death.
How gracious and how perfecting a grace
    Must patience be on which those others wait:
Faith with suspended rapture in her face,
    Hope pale and careful hand in hand with fear,
Love—ah, good love who would not antedate
    God's Will, but saith, Good is it to be here.

LORD, grant us grace to rest upon Thy word,
    To rest in hope until we see Thy Face;
To rest thro' toil unruffled and unstirred,
    Lord, grant us grace.

Gifts and Graces.

This burden and this heat wear on apace:
Night comes, when sweeter than night's singing
    bird
Will swell the silence of our ended race.

Ah, songs which flesh and blood have never heard
    And cannot hear, songs of the silent place
Where rest remains ! Lord, slake our hope deferred,
    Lord, grant us grace.

THE WORLD.
SELF-DESTRUCTION.

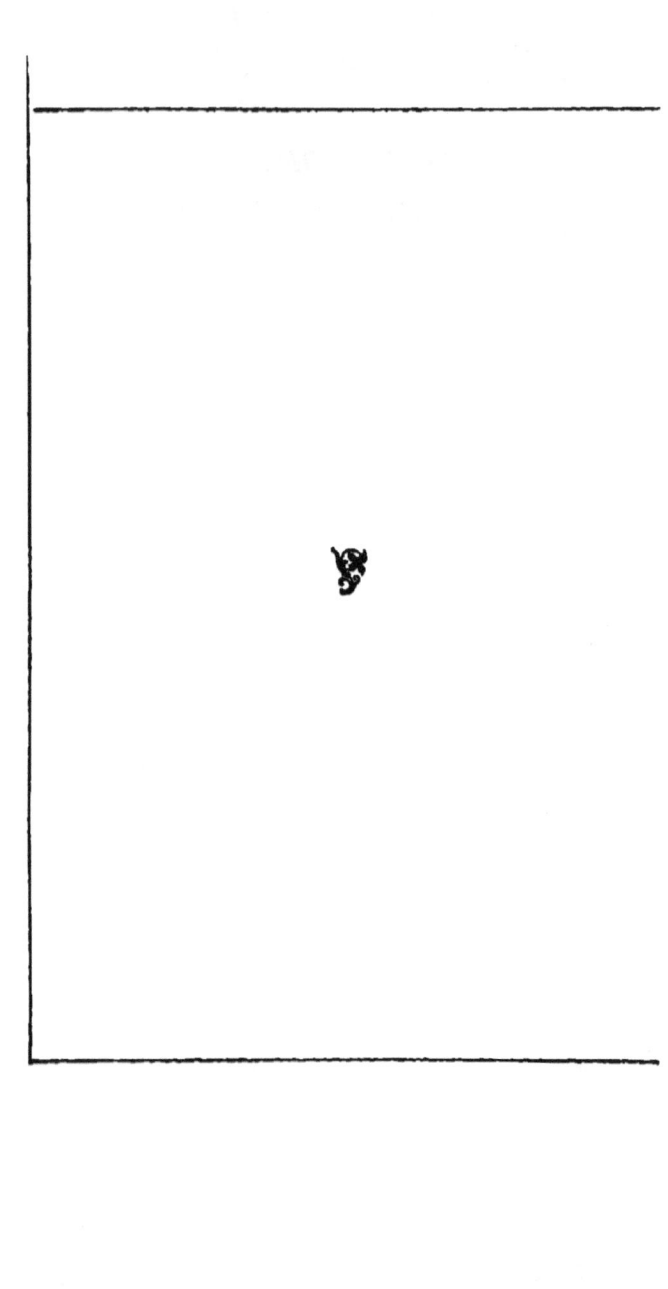

"A vain Shadow."

THE world,—what a world, ah me!
  Mouldy, worm-eaten, grey:
Vain as a leaf from a tree,
  As a fading day,
As veriest vanity,
  As the froth and the spray
Of the hollow-billowed sea,
As what was and shall not be,
  As what is and passes away.

"Lord, save us, we perish."

LORD, seek us, O Lord, find us
  In Thy patient care;
Be Thy Love before, behind us,
  Round us, everywhere:
Lest the god of this world blind us,
  Lest he speak us fair,
Lest he forge a chain to bind us,
  Lest he bait a snare.

Turn not from us, call to mind us,
   Find, embrace us, bear;
Be Thy Love before, behind us,
   Round us, everywhere.

WHAT is this above thy head,
   O Man?—
The World, all overspread
With pearls and golden rays
And gems ablaze;
A sight which day and night
   Fills an eye's span.

What is this beneath thy feet,
   O Saint?—
The World, a nauseous sweet
Puffed up and perishing;
A hollow thing,
A lie, a vanity,
   Tinsel and paint.

What is she while time is time,
   O Man?—
In a perpetual prime
Beauty and youth she hath;
And her footpath
Breeds flowers thro' dancing hours
   Since time began.

While time lengthens what is she,
　　O Saint?—
Nought: yea, all men shall see
How she is nought at all,
When her death-pall
Of fire ends their desire
　　And brands her taint.

Ah, poor Man, befooled and slow
　　And faint!
Ah, poorest Man, if so
Thou turn thy back on bliss
And choose amiss!
For thou art choosing now:
　　Sinner,—or Saint.

Babylon the Great.

FOUL is she and ill-favoured, set askew:
　　Gaze not upon her till thou dream her fair,
　Lest she should mesh thee in her wanton hair,
Adept in arts grown old yet ever new.
Her heart lusts not for love, but thro' and thro'
　For blood, as spotted panther lusts in lair;
　No wine is in her cup, but filth is there
Unutterable, with plagues hid out of view.
Gaze not upon her, for her dancing whirl
　Turns giddy the fixed gazer presently:
　Gaze not upon her, lest thou be as she
　　When, at the far end of her long desire,
Her scarlet vest and gold and gem and pearl
　　And she amid her pomp are set on fire.

"Standing afar off for the fear of her torment."

IS this the end? is there no end but this?
   Yea, none beside:
  No other end for pride
And foulness and besottedness.

Hath she no friend? hath she no clinging friend?
   Nay, none at all;
  Who stare upon her fall
Quake for themselves with hair on end.

Will she be done away? vanish away?
   Yea, like a dream;
  Yea, like the shades that seem
Somewhat, and lo! are nought by day.

Alas for her amid man's helpless moan,
   Alas for her!
  She hath no comforter:
In solitude of fire she sits alone.

"O Lucifer, Son of the Morning!"

OH fallen star! a darkened light,
   A glory hurtled from its car,
Self-blasted from the holy height:
   Oh fallen star!

Fallen beyond earth's utmost bar,
  Beyond return, beyond far sight
   Of outmost glimmering nebular.

The World. Self=Destruction.

Now blackness, which once walked in white;
 Now death, whose life once glowed afar;
Oh son of dawn that loved the night,
 Oh fallen star!

LAS, alas! for the self-destroyed
 Vanish as images from a glass,
Sink down and die down by hope unbuoyed :—
 Alas, alas!

Who shall stay their ruinous mass?
Besotted, reckless, possessed, decoyed,
 They hurry to the dolorous pass.

Saints fall a-weeping who would have joyed,
 Sore they weep for a glory that was,
For a fulness emptied into the void,
 Alas, alas!

S froth on the face of the deep,
 As foam on the crest of the sea,
As dreams at the waking of sleep,
 As gourd of a day and a night,
As harvest that no man shall reap,
 As vintage that never shall be,
Is hope if it cling not aright,
 O my God, unto Thee.

*"Where their worm dieth not, and the fire is
not quenched."*

IN tempest and storm blackness of darkness
for ever,
A fire unextinguished, a worm's indestructible
swarm ;
Where no hope shall ever be more, and love
shall be never,
In tempest and storm;
Where the form of all things is fashionless,
void of all form;
Where from death that severeth all, the soul
cannot sever
In tempest and storm.

TOLL, bell, toll. For hope is flying
Sighing from the earthbound soul:
Life is sighing, life is dying:
Toll, bell, toll.

Gropes in its own grave the mole
Wedding darkness, undescrying,
Tending to no different goal.

Self-slain soul, in vain thy sighing:
Self-slain, who should make thee whole?
Vain the clamour of thy crying:
Toll, bell, toll.

DIVERS WORLDS.
TIME AND ETERNITY.

DIVERS WORLDS. TIME AND ETERNITY.

EARTH has clear call of daily bells,
A chancel-vault of gloom and star,
  A rapture where the anthems are,
A thunder when the organ swells:
Alas, man's daily life—what else?—
Is out of tune with daily bells.

While Paradise accords the chimes
  Of Earth and Heaven, its patient pause
  Is rest fulfilling music's laws.
Saints sit and gaze, where oftentimes
Precursive flush of morning climbs
And air vibrates with coming chimes.

"Escape to the Mountain."

I PEERED within, and saw a world of sin;
  Upward, and saw a world of righteousness;
Downward, and saw darkness and flame begin
  Which no man can express.

I girt me up, I gat me up to flee
From face of darkness and devouring flame:
And fled I had, but guilt is loading me
With dust of death and shame.

Yet still the light of righteousness beams pure,
Beams to me from the world of far-off day:—
Lord, Who hast called them happy that endure,
Lord, make me such as they.

I LIFT mine eyes to see: earth vanisheth.
I lift up wistful eyes and bend my knee:
Trembling, bowed down, and face to face with
Death,
I lift mine eyes to see.

Lo, what I see is Death that shadows me:
Yet whilst I, seeing, draw a shuddering breath,
Death like a mist grows rare perceptibly.

Beyond the darkness light, beyond the scathe
Healing, beyond the Cross a palm-branch tree,
Beyond Death Life, on evidence of faith:
I lift mine eyes to see.

"Yet a little while."

HEAVEN is not far, tho' far the sky
Overarching earth and main.
It takes not long to live and die,
Die, revive, and rise again.
Not long: how long? Oh, long re-echoing song!
O Lord, how long?

"Behold, it was very good."

ALL things are fair, if we had eyes to see
How first God made them goodly everywhere:
And goodly still in Paradise they be,—
All things are fair.

O Lord, the solemn heavens Thy praise declare;
The multi-fashioned saints bring praise to Thee,
As doves fly home and cast away their care.

As doves on divers branches of their tree,
Perched high or low, sit all contented there
Not mourning any more; in each degree
All things are fair.

❖

"Whatsoever is right, that shall ye receive."

WHEN all the overwork of life
Is finished once, and fallen asleep
We shrink no more beneath the knife,
But having sown prepare to reap;
Delivered from the crossway rough,
Delivered from the thorny scourge,
Delivered from the tossing surge,
Then shall we find—(please God!)—it is enough?

Not in this world of hope deferred,
This world of perishable stuff;
Eye hath not seen, nor ear hath heard,
Nor heart conceived that full "enough":
Here moans the separating sea,
Here harvests fail, here breaks the heart;
There God shall join and no man part,
All one in Christ, so one—(please God!)—with me.

Divers Worlds. Time and Eternity.

THIS near-at-hand land breeds pain by measure:
That far-away land overflows with treasure
Of heaped-up good pleasure.

Our land that we see is befouled by evil:
The land that we see not makes mirth and revel,
Far from death and devil.

This land hath for music sobbing and sighing:
That land hath soft speech and sweet soft replying
Of all loves undying.

This land hath for pastime errors and follies:
That land hath unending unflagging solace
Of full-chanted "Holies."

Up and away, call the Angels to us;
Come to our home where no foes pursue us,
And no tears bedew us;

Where that which riseth sets again never,
Where that which springeth flows in a river
For ever and ever;

Where harvest justifies labour of sowing,
Where that which budded comes to the blowing
Sweet beyond your knowing.

Come and laugh with us, sing in our singing;
Come, yearn no more, but rest in your clinging.
See what we are bringing;

Crowns like our own crowns, robes for your
        wearing ;
For love of you we kiss them in bearing,
        All good with you sharing :

Over you gladdening, in you delighting ;
Come from your famine, your failure, your fighting ;
        Come to full wrong-righting.

Come, where all balm is garnered to ease you ;
Come, where all beauty is spread out to please you ;
        Come, gaze upon Jesu.

"Was Thy Wrath against the Sea ?"

THE sea laments with unappeasable
  Hankering wail of loss,
    Lifting its hands on high and passing by
      Out of the lovely light :
No foambow any more may crest that swell
  Of clamorous waves which toss ;
    Lifting its hands on high it passes by
      From light into the night.
Peace, peace, thou sea ! God's wisdom worketh
        well,
  Assigns it crown or cross :
    Lift we all hands on high, and passing by
      Attest : God doeth right.

"And there was no more Sea."

VOICES from above and from beneath,
 Voices of creation near and far,
Voices out of life and out of death,
   Out of measureless space,
  Sun, moon, star,
    In oneness of contentment offering praise.

Heaven and earth and sea jubilant,
  Jubilant all things that dwell therein;
Filled to fullest overflow they chant,
   Still roll onward, swell,
  Still begin,
    Never flagging praise interminable.

Thou who must fall silent in a while,
  Chant thy sweetest, gladdest, best, at once;
Sun thyself to-day, keep peace and smile;
   By love upward send
  Orisons,
    Accounting love thy lot and love thine end.

ROSES on a brier,
   Pearls from out the bitter sea,
Such is earth's desire
  However pure it be.

Neither bud nor brier,
  Neither pearl nor brine for me:
Be stilled, my long desire;
  There shall be no more sea.

Be stilled, my passionate heart;
    Old earth shall end, new earth shall be:
Be still, and earn thy part
    Where shall be no more sea.

WE are of those who tremble at Thy word;
    Who faltering walk in darkness toward
        our close
Of mortal life, by terrors curbed and spurred:
    We are of those.

We journey to that land which no man knows
Who any more can make his voice be heard
    Above the clamour of our wants and woes.

Not ours the hearts Thy loftiest love hath stirred,
    Not such as we Thy lily and Thy rose:—
Yet, Hope of those who hope with hope deferred,
    We are of those.

"Awake, thou that sleepest."

THE night is far spent, the day is at hand:
    Let us therefore cast off the works of darkness,
    And let us put on the armour of light.
    Night for the dead in their stiffness and starkness!
    Day for the living who mount in their might
Out of their graves to the beautiful land.

Far, far away lies the beautiful land :
  Mount on wide wings of exceeding desire,
    Mount, look not back, mount to life and to light,
  Mount by the gleam of your lamps all on fire
    Up from the dead men and up from the night.
The night is far spent, the day is at hand.

WE know not when, we know not where,
  We know not what that world will be;
But this we know : it will be fair
  To see.

With heart athirst and thirsty face
  We know and know not what shall be :
Christ Jesus bring us of His grace
  To see.

Christ Jesus bring us of His grace,
  Beyond all prayers our hope can pray,
One day to see Him face to Face,
  One day.

"I will lift up mine eyes unto the hills."

WHEN sick of life and all the world—
  How sick of all desire but Thee !—
I lift mine eyes up to the hills,
  Eyes of my heart that see,
I see beyond all death and ills
Refreshing green for heart and eyes,
The golden streets and gateways pearled,
  The trees of Paradise.

"There is a time for all things," saith
The Word of Truth, Thyself the Word;
And many things Thou reasonest of:
　A time for hope deferred,
But time is now for grief and fears;
A time for life, but now is death;
Oh, when shall be the time of love
　When Thou shalt wipe our tears?

Then the new Heavens and Earth shall be
Where righteousness shall dwell indeed;
There shall be no more blight, nor need,
　Nor barrier of the sea;
No sun and moon alternating,
For God shall be the Light thereof;
No sorrow more, no death, no sting,
　For God Who reigns is Love.

"Then whose shall those things be?"

OH what is earth, that we should build
　Our houses here, and seek concealed
Poor treasure, and add field to field,
And heap to heap, and store to store,
Still grasping more and seeking more,
While step by step Death nears the door?

"His Banner over me was Love."

IN that world we weary to attain,
  Love's furled banner floats at large unfurled:
There is no more doubt and no more pain
  In that world.

There are gems and gold and inlets pearled;
There the verdure fadeth not again;
  There no clinging tendrils droop uncurled.

Here incessant tides stir up the main,
  Stormy miry depths aloft are hurled:
There is no more sea, or storm, or stain,
  In that world.

BELOVED, yield thy time to God, for He
  Will make eternity thy recompense;
Give all thy substance for His Love, and be
  Beatified past earth's experience.
Serve Him in bonds, until He set thee free;
  Serve Him in dust, until He lift thee thence;
Till death be swallowed up in victory
  When the great trumpet sounds to bid thee hence.
Shall setting day win day that will not set?
  Poor price wert thou to spend thyself for Christ,
  Had not His wealth thy poverty sufficed:
    Yet since He makes His garden of thy clod,
Water thy lily, rose, or violet,
    And offer up thy sweetness unto God.

TIME seems not short:
　　If so I call to mind
　　Its vast prerogative to loose or bind,
And bear and strike amort
　　All humankind.

Time seems not long:
　　If I peer out and see
　　Sphere within sphere, time in eternity,
And hear the alternate song
　　Cry endlessly.

Time greatly short,
　　O time so briefly long,
　　Yea, time sole battle-ground of right and
　　　　wrong:
Art thou a time for sport
　　And for a song?

❖

THE half moon shows a face of plaintive
　　　　sweetness
　　Ready and poised to wax or wane;
A fire of pale desire in incompleteness,
　　Tending to pleasure or to pain:—
Lo, while we gaze she rolleth on in fleetness
　　To perfect loss or perfect gain.

Half bitterness we know, we know half sweetness;
　　This world is all on wax, on wane:
When shall completeness round time's incom-
　　　　pleteness,
　　Fulfilling joy, fulfilling pain?—
Lo, while we ask, life rolleth on in fleetness
　　To finished loss or finished gain.

"As the Doves to their windows."

THEY throng from the east and the west,
  The north and the south, with a song;
To golden abodes of their rest
  They throng.

Eternity stretches out long:
Time, brief at its worst or its best,
  Will quit them of ruin and wrong.

A rainbow aloft for their crest,
  A palm for their weakness made strong!
As doves breast all winds to their nest,
  They throng.

OH knell of a passing time,
  Will it never cease to chime?
Oh stir of the tedious sea,
Will it never cease to be?
Yea, when night and when day,
Moon and sun, pass away.

Surely the sun burns low,
The moon makes ready to go,
Broad ocean ripples to waste,
Time is running in haste,
Night is numbered, and day
Numbered to pass away.

Divers Worlds. Time and Eternity.

TIME passeth away with its pleasure and pain,
　Its garlands of cypress and bay,
With wealth and with want, with a balm and
　　a bane,
　Time passeth away.

　Eternity cometh to stay,
Eternity stayeth to go not again;
　Eternity barring the way,

Arresting all courses of planet or main,
　Arresting who plan or who pray,
Arresting creation: while grand in its wane
　Time passeth away.

"The Earth shall tremble at the Look of Him."

TREMBLE, thou earth, at the Presence of the
　　Lord
　Whose Will conceived thee and brought thee to
　　the birth,
Always, everywhere, thy Lord to be adored:
　Tremble, thou earth.

　Wilt thou laugh time away in music and mirth?
Time hath days of pestilence, hath days of a sword,
　Hath days of hunger and thirst in desolate dearth.

Till eternity wake up the multicord
　Thrilled harp of heaven, and breathe full its
　　organ's girth
For joy of heaven and infinite reward,
　Tremble, thou earth.

TIME lengthening, in the lengthening seemeth
    long:
But ended Time will seem a little space,
A little while from morn to evensong,
A little while that ran a rapid race;
  A little while, when once Eternity
  Denies proportion to the other's pace.
Eternity to be and be and be,
  Ever beginning, never ending still,
  Still undiminished far as thought can see;
Farther than thought can see, by dint of will
  Strung up and strained and shooting like a star
  Past utmost bound of everlasting hill:
Eternity unswaddled, without bar,
  Finishing sequence in its awful sum;
  Eternity still rolling forth its car,
Eternity still here and still to come.

"All Flesh is Grass."

SO brief a life, and then an endless life
  Or endless death;
So brief a life, then endless peace or strife:
  Whoso considereth
How man but like a flower
  Or shoot of grass
Blooms an hour,
  Well may sigh "Alas!"

So brief a life, and then an endless grief
  Or endless joy;
So brief a life, then ruin or relief:
  What solace, what annoy
Of Time needs dwelling on?
  It is, it was,
It is done,
  While we sigh "Alas!"

Yet saints are singing in a happy hope
  Forecasting pleasure,
Bright eyes of faith enlarging all their scope;
  Saints love beyond Time's measure:
Where love is, there is bliss
  That will not pass;
Where love is,
  Dies away "Alas!"

HEAVEN'S chimes are slow, but sure to strike
    at last:
Earth's sands are slow, but surely dropping thro':
And much we have to suffer, much to do,
  Before the time be past.

Chimes that keep time are neither slow nor fast:
  Not many are the numbered sands nor few:
  A time to suffer, and a time to do,
    And then the time is past.

"There remaineth therefore a Rest to the
People of God."

REST remains when all is done,
    Work and vigil, prayer and fast,
All fulfilled from first to last,
All the length of time gone past
And eternity begun !

Fear and hope and chastening rod
    Urge us on the narrow way:
Bear we now as best we may
Heat and burden of to-day,
Struggling, panting up to God.

PARTING after parting,
    Sore loss and gnawing pain:
Meeting grows half a sorrow
    Because of parting again.
When shall the day break
    That these things shall not be?
When shall new earth be ours
    Without a sea,
And time that is not time
    But eternity?

To meet, worth living for;
  Worth dying for, to meet;
To meet, worth parting for,
  Bitter forgot in sweet:
To meet, worth parting before
  Never to part more.

"They put their trust in Thee, and were not confounded."

I.

TOGETHER once, but never more
  While Time and Death run out their runs:
Tho' sundered now as shore from shore,
  Together once.

Nor rising suns, nor setting suns,
Nor life renewed which springtide bore,
  Make one again Death's sundered ones.

Eternity holds rest in store,
  Holds hope of long reunions:
But holds it what they hungered for
  Together once?

II.

Whatso it be, howso it be, Amen.
  Blessed it is, believing, not to see.
Now God knows all that is; and we shall, then,
  Whatso it be.

God's Will is best for man whose will is free.
God's Will is better to us, yea, than ten
   Desires whereof He holds and weighs the key.

Amid her household cares He guides the wren,
   He guards the shifty mouse from poverty;
He knows all wants, allots each where and when,
   Whatso it be.

SHORT is time, and only time is bleak;
   Gauge the exceeding height thou hast to
   climb:
Long eternity is nigh to seek:
   Short is time.

Time is shortening with the wintry rime:
Pray and watch and pray, girt up and meek;
   Praying, watching, praying, chime by chime.

Pray by silence if thou canst not speak:
   Time is shortening; pray on till the prime:
Time is shortening; soul, fulfil thy week:
   Short is time.

For Each.

MY harvest is done, its promise is ended,
   Weak and watery sets the sun,
Day and night in one mist are blended,
   My harvest is done.

Long while running, how short when run,
Time to eternity has descended,
 Timeless eternity has begun.

Was it the narrow way that I wended?
 Snares and pits was it mine to shun?
The scythe has fallen, so long suspended,
 My harvest is done.

For All.

MAN'S harvest is past, his summer is ended,
 Hope and fear are finished at last,
Day hath descended, night hath ascended,
 Man's harvest is past.

Time is fled that fleeted so fast:
All the unmended remains unmended,
 The perfect, perfect: all lots are cast.

Waiting till earth and ocean be rended,
 Waiting for call of the trumpet blast,
Each soul at goal of that way it wended,—
 Man's harvest is past.

NEW JERUSALEM AND ITS CITIZENS.

—٠٠—

"The holy City, New Jerusalem."

JERUSALEM is built of gold,
  Of crystal, pearl, and gem:
Oh fair thy lustres manifold,
  Thou fair Jerusalem !
Thy citizens who walk in white
Have nought to do with day or night,
And drink the river of delight.

Jerusalem makes melody
  For simple joy of heart ;
An organ of full compass she,
  One-tuned thro' every part:
While not to day or night belong
Her matins and her evensong,
The one thanksgiving of her throng.

Jerusalem a garden is,
  A garden of delight;
Leaf, flower, and fruit make fair her trees,
  Which see not day or night:
Beside her River clear and calm
The Tree of Life grows with the Palm,
For triumph and for food and balm.

Jerusalem, where song nor gem
  Nor fruit nor waters cease,
God bring us to Jerusalem,
  God bring us home in peace;
The strong who stand, the weak who fall,
The first and last, the great and small,
Home one by one, home one and all.

WHEN wickedness is broken as a tree
  Paradise comes to light, ah holy land!
Whence death has vanished like a shifting sand,
And barrenness is banished with the sea.
Its bulwarks are salvation fully manned,
  All gems it hath for glad variety,
  And pearls for pureness radiant glimmeringly,
And gold for grandeur where all good is grand.
An inner ring of saints meets linked above,
  And linked of angels is an outer ring;
    For voice of waters or for thunders' voice
    Lo! harps and songs wherewith all saints
      rejoice,
  And all the trembling there of any string
Is but a trembling of enraptured love.

JERUSALEM of fire
  And gold and pearl and gem,
Saints flock to fill thy choir,
  Jerusalem.

Lo, thrones thou hast for them;
Desirous they desire
Thy harp, thy diadem,

Thy bridal white attire,
A palm-branch from thy stem:
Thy holiness their hire,
Jerusalem.

"She shall be brought unto the King."

THE King's Daughter is all glorious within,
Her clothing of wrought gold sets forth her
bliss;
Where the endless choruses of heaven begin
The King's Daughter is;

Perfect her notes in the perfect harmonies;
With tears wiped away, no conscience of sin,
Loss forgotten and sorrowful memories;

Alight with Cherubin, afire with Seraphin,
Lily for pureness, rose for charities,
With joy won and with joy evermore to win,
The King's Daughter is.

WHO is this that cometh up not alone
  From the fiery-flying-serpent wilderness,
Leaning upon her own Beloved One:
 Who is this?

Lo, the King of kings' daughter, a high princess,
Going home as bride to her Husband's Throne,
 Virgin queen in perfected loveliness.

Her eyes a dove's eyes and her voice a dove's moan,
 She shows like a full moon for heavenliness:
Eager saints and angels ask in heaven's zone,
 Who is this?

WHO sits with the King in His Throne?
  Not a slave but a Bride,
 With this King of all Greatness and Grace
  Who reigns not alone;
His Glory her glory, where glorious she glows at
  His side
 Who sits with the King in His Throne.

She came from dim uttermost depths which no
  Angel hath known,
Leviathan's whirlpool and Dragon's dominion
  worldwide,
 From the frost or the fire to Paradisiacal zone.
Lo, she is fair as a dove, silvery, golden, dove-eyed:
 Lo, Dragon laments and Death laments, for
  their prey is flown:
She dwells in the Vision of Peace, and her
  peace shall abide
 Who sits with the King in His Throne.

Antipas.

HIDDEN from the darkness of our mortal
    sight,
Hidden in the Paradise of lovely light,
Hidden in God's Presence, worshipped face to face,
Hidden in the sanctuary of Christ's embrace.
Up, O Wills! to track him home among the
    bless'd;
Up, O Hearts! to know him in the joy of rest;
Where no darkness more shall hide him from
    our sight,
Where we shall be love with love, and light with
    light,
Worshipping our God together face to face,
Wishless in the sanctuary of Christ's embrace.

"Beautiful for situation."

A LOVELY city in a lovely land,
    Whose citizens are lovely, and whose King
Is Very Love; to Whom all Angels sing;
To Whom all saints sing crowned, their sacred band
Saluting Love with palm-branch in their hand:
    Thither all doves on gold or silver wing
    Flock home thro' agate windows glistering
Set wide, and where pearl gates wide open stand.
A bower of roses is not half so sweet,
    A cave of diamonds doth not glitter so,
      Nor Lebanon is fruitful set thereby:
      And thither thou, beloved, and thither I
    May set our heart and set our face and go,
Faint yet pursuing, home on tireless feet.

New Jerusalem and its Citizens.

LORD, by what inconceivable dim road
 Thou leadest man on footsore pilgrimage!
Weariness is his rest from stage to stage,
Brief halting-places are his sole abode.
Onward he fares thro' rivers overflowed,
 Thro' deserts where all doleful creatures rage;
 Onward from year to year, from age to age,
He groans and totters onward with his load.
Behold how inconceivable his way;
 How tenfold inconceivable the goal,
 His goal of hope deferred, his promised peace:
 Yea, but behold him sitting down at ease,
Refreshed in body and refreshed in soul,
At rest from labour on the Sabbath Day.

"As cold waters to a thirsty soul, so is good
news from a far country."

" GOLDEN haired, lily white,
 Will you pluck me lilies?
Or will you show me where they grow,
 Show where the limpid rill is?
But is your hair of gold or light,
 And is your foot of flake or fire,
And have you wings rolled up from sight
 And songs to slake desire?"

"I pluck fresh flowers of Paradise,
  Lilies and roses red,
A bending sceptre for my hand,
  A crown to crown my head.
I sing my songs, I pluck my flowers
  Sweet-scented from their fragrant trees;
I sing, we sing, amid the bowers
  And gather palm-branches."

"Is there a path to Heaven
  My stumbling foot may tread?
And will you show that way to go,
  That bower and blossom bed?"
"The path to Heaven is steep and straight
  And scorched, but ends in shade of trees,
Where yet a while we sing and wait
  And gather palm-branches."

CAST down but not destroyed, chastened not
    slain:
  Thy Saints have lived that life, but how can I?
  I, who thro' dread of death do daily die
By daily foretaste of an unfelt pain.
Lo, I depart who shall not come again;
  Lo, as a shadow I am flitting by;
  As a leaf trembling, as a wheel I fly,
While death flies faster and my flight is vain.

Chastened not slain, cast down but not destroyed:—
  If thus Thy Saints have struggled home to
      peace,
    Why should not I take heart to be as they?
    They too pent passions in a house of clay,
  Fear and desire, and pangs and ecstasies;
Yea, thus they joyed who now are overjoyed.

LIFT up thine eyes to seek the invisible:
    Stir up thy heart to choose the still unseen:
  Strain up thy hope in glad perpetual green
To scale the exceeding height where all saints
      dwell.
—Saints, is it well with you?—Yea, it is well.—
  Where they have reaped, by faith kneel thou
      to glean:
  Because they stooped so low to reap, they lean
Now over golden harps unspeakable.
—But thou purblind and deafened, knowest thou
  Those glorious beauties unexperienced
    By ear or eye or by heart hitherto?—
I know Whom I have trusted: wherefore now
  All amiable, accessible tho' fenced,
    Golden Jerusalem floats full in view.

"Love is strong as Death."

AS flames that consume the mountains, as winds
    that coerce the sea,
Thy men of renown show forth Thy might in
    the clutch of death:
Down they go into silence, yet the Trump of the
    Jubilee
    Swells not Thy praise as swells it the breathless
      pause of their breath.

What is the flame of their fire, if so I may catch
    the flame;
    What the strength of their strength, if also I may
      wax strong?
The flaming fire of their strength is the love of
    Jesu's Name,
    In Whom their death is life, their silence utters
      a song.

"Let them rejoice in their beds."

CRIMSON as the rubies, crimson as the roses,
    Crimson as the sinking sun,
Singing on his crimsoned bed each saint reposes,
    Fought his fight, his battle won;
Till the rosy east the day of days discloses,
    All his work, save waiting, done.

Far above the stars, while underneath the daisies,
    Resting, for his race is run,
Unto Thee his heart each quiet saint upraises,
    God the Father, Spirit, Son;
Unto Thee his heart, unto Thee his praises,
    O Lord God, the Three in One.

SLAIN in their high places: fallen on rest
  Where the eternal peace lights up their faces,
In God's sacred acre breast to breast:—
  Slain in their high places.

From all tribes, all families, all races,
Gathered home together; east or west
  Sending home its tale of gifts and graces.

Twine, oh twine, heaven's amaranth for their crest,
  Raise their praise while home their triumph paces;
Kings by their own King of kings confessed,
  Slain in their high places.

"What hath God wrought!"

THE shout of a King is among them. One
    day may I be
Of that perfect communion of lovers contented
    and free
In the land that is very far off, and far off from
    the sea.

The shout of the King is among them. One
    King and one song,
One thunder of manifold voices harmonious and
    strong,
One King and one love, and one shout of one
    worshipping throng.

"Before the Throne, and before the Lamb."

AS the voice of many waters all saints sing
    as one,
As the voice of an unclouded thundering;
Unswayed by the changing moon and unswayed
    by the sun,
  As the voice of many waters all saints sing.

Circling round the rainbow of their perfect ring,
Twelve thousand times twelve thousand voices in
    unison
  Swell the triumph, swell the praise of Christ
    the King.

Where raiment is white of blood-steeped linen
    slowly spun,
  Where crowns are golden of Love's own
    largessing,
Where eternally the ecstasy is but begun,
  As the voice of many waters all saints sing.

"He shall go no more out."

ONCE within, within for evermore:
    There the long beatitudes begin:
Overflows the still unwasting store,
  Once within.

Left without are death and doubt and sin;
All man wrestled with and all he bore,
  Man who saved his life, skin after skin.

Blow the trumpet-blast unheard before,
  Shout the unheard-of shout for these who win,
These, who cast their crowns on Heaven's high
    floor
Once within.

YEA, blessed and holy is he that hath part in
  the First Resurrection!
  We mark well his bulwarks, we set up his
    tokens, we gaze, even we,
On this lustre of God and of Christ, this creature
  of flawless perfection:
  Yea, blessed and holy is he.

  But what? an offscouring of earth, a wreck
    from the turbulent sea,
A bloodstone unflinchingly hewn for the Temple's
  eternal erection,
  One scattered and peeled, one sifted and chas-
    tened and scourged and set free?

Yea, this is that worshipful stone of the Wise
    Master Builder's election,
  Yea, this is that King and that Priest where all
    Hallows bow down the knee,
Yea, this man set nigh to the Throne is Jonathan
  of David's delection,
  Yea, blessed and holy is he.

THE joy of Saints, like incense turned to fire
    In golden censers, soars acceptable;
And high their heavenly hallelujahs swell
Desirous still with still-fulfilled desire.
Sweet thrill the harpstrings of the heavenly choir,
    Most sweet their voice while love is all they tell;
    Where love is all in all, and all is well
Because their work is love and love their hire.
All robed in white and all with palm in hand,
    Crowns too they have of gold and thrones of gold;
        The street is golden which their feet have trod,
Or on a sea of glass and fire they stand:
    And none of them is young, and none is old,
    Except as perfect by the Will of God.

❖

WHAT are these lovely ones, yea, what are
        these?
    Lo, these are they who for pure love of Christ
Stripped off the trammels of soft silken ease,
    Beggaring themselves betimes, to be sufficed
Throughout heaven's one eternal day of peace:
    By golden streets, thro' gates of pearl unpriced,
They entered on the joys that will not cease,
    And found again all firstfruits sacrificed.
And wherefore have you harps, and wherefore palms,
    And wherefore crowns, O ye who walk in white?
Because our happy hearts are chanting psalms,
    Endless Te Deum for the ended fight;
While thro' the everlasting lapse of calms
    We cast our crowns before the Lamb our Might.

❖

"The General Assembly and Church of the Firstborn."

BRING me to see, Lord, bring me yet to see
　Those nations of Thy glory and Thy grace
Who splendid in Thy splendour worship Thee.
Light in all eyes, content in every face,
　Raptures and voices one while manifold,
　Love and are well-beloved the ransomed race:—
Great mitred priests, great kings in crowns of gold,
　Patriarchs who head the army of their sons,
　Matrons and mothers by their own extolled,
Wise and most harmless holy little ones,
　Virgins who, making merry, lead the dance,
　Full-breathed victorious racers from all runs,
Home-comers out of every change and chance,
　Hermits restored to social neighbourhood,
　Aspects which reproduce One Countenance,
Life-losers with their losses all made good,
　All blessed hungry and athirst sufficed,
　All who bore crosses round the Holy Rood,
Friends, brethren, sisters, of Lord Jesus Christ.

"Every one that is perfect shall be as his master."

HOW can one man, how can all men,
　How can we be like St. Paul,
Like St. John, or like St. Peter,
　Like the least of all
　Blessed Saints? for we are small.

Love can make us like St. Peter,
  Love can make us like St. Paul,
Love can make us like the blessed
  Bosom friend of all,
  Great St. John, tho' we are small.

Love which clings and trusts and worships,
  Love which rises from a fall,
Love which, prompting glad obedience,
  Labours most of all,
  Love makes great the great and small.

❖

" AS dying, and behold we live!"
    So live the Saints while time is flying;
Make all they make, give all they give,
  As dying;
  Bear all they bear without replying;
They grieve as tho' they did not grieve,
  Uplifting praise with prayer and sighing.

Patient thro' life's long-drawn reprieve,
  Aloof from strife, at peace from crying,
The morrow to its day they leave,
  As dying.   ❖

"So great a cloud of Witnesses."

I THINK of the saints I have known, and
    lift up mine eyes
To the far-away home of beautiful Paradise,
Where the song of saints gives voice to an un-
    dividing sea
On whose plain their feet stand firm while they
    keep their jubilee.

As the sound of waters their voice, as the sound
of thunderings,
While they all at once rejoice, while all sing and
while each one sings;
Where more saints flock in, and more, and yet
more, and again yet more,
And not one turns back to depart thro' the open
entrance-door.

O sights of our lovely earth, O sound of our
earthly sea,
Speak to me of Paradise, of all blessed saints to me :
Or keep silence touching them, and speak to my
heart alone
Of the Saint of saints, the King of kings, the
Lamb on the Throne.

UR Mothers, lovely women pitiful;
  Our Sisters, gracious in their life and death;
To us each unforgotten memory saith :
"Learn as we learned in life's sufficient school,
Work as we worked in patience of our rule,
  Walk as we walked, much less by sight than faith,
  Hope as we hoped, despite our slips and scathe,
Fearful in joy and confident in dule."
I know not if they see us or can see ;
  But if they see us in our painful day,
    How looking back to earth from Paradise
    Do tears not gather in those loving eyes?—
  Ah, happy eyes! whose tears are wiped away
Whether or not you bear to look on me.

SAFE where I cannot lie yet,
  Safe where I hope to lie too,
Safe from the fume and the fret;
  You, and you,
Whom I never forget.

Safe from the frost and the snow,
  Safe from the storm and the sun,
Safe where the seeds wait to grow
  One by one
And to come back in blow.

"Is it well with the child?"

LYING a-dying.
  Have done with vain sighing:
Life not lost but treasured,
God Almighty pleasured,
God's daughter fetched and carried,
Christ's bride betrothed and married.
Our tender little dove
Meek-eyed and simple,
Our love goes home to Love:
There shall she walk in white,
Where God shall be the Light,
And God the Temple.

DEAR Angels and dear disembodied Saints
  Unseen around us, worshipping in rest,
May wonder that man's heart so often faints
 And his steps lag along the heavenly quest,
What while his foolish fancy moulds and paints
 A fonder hope than all they prove for best;
A lying hope which undermines and taints
 His soul, as sin and sloth make manifest.
Sloth, and a lie, and sin: shall these suffice
 The unfathomable heart of craving man,
  That heart which being a deep calls to the deep?
Behold how many like us rose and ran
  When Christ, life-giver, roused them from their
   sleep
To rise and run and rest in Paradise!

"To every seed his own body."

BONE to his bone, grain to his grain of dust:
  A numberless reunion shall make whole
 Each blessed body for its blessed soul,
Refashioning the aspects of the just.
Each saint who died must live afresh, and must
 Ascend resplendent in the aureole
 Of his own proper glory to his goal,
As seeds their proper bodies all upthrust.
Each with his own not with another's grace,
 Each with his own not with another's heart,
Each with his own not with another's face,
Each dove-like soul mounts to his proper place :—
 O faces unforgotten! if to part
Wrung sore, what will it be to re-embrace?

New Jerusalem and its Citizens.

"What good shall my life do me?"

HAVE dead men long to wait?—

There is a certain term
For their bodies to the worm
And their souls at heaven gate.
Dust to dust, clod to clod,
These precious things of God,
Trampled underfoot by man
And beast the appointed years.—

Their longest life was but a span
For change and smiles and tears.
Is it worth while to live,
Rejoice and grieve,
Hope, fear, and die?
Man with man, truth with lie,
The slow show dwindles by:
At last what shall we have
Besides a grave?—

Lies and shows no more,
No fear, no pain,
But after hope and sleep
Dear joys again.
Those who sowed shall reap:
Those who bore
The Cross shall wear the Crown:
Those who clomb the steep
There shall sit down.

The Shepherd of the sheep
Feeds His flock there,
In watered pastures fair
They rest and leap.
"Is it worth while to live?"
Be of good cheer:
Love casts out fear:
Rise up, achieve.

✤

SONGS FOR STRANGERS AND PILGRIMS.

✤

SONGS FOR STRANGERS AND PILGRIMS.

"Iber Seed; It shall bruise thy head."

ASTONISHED Heaven looked on when man
    was made,
When fallen man reproved seemed half for-
    given; .
Surely that oracle of hope first said,
    Astonished Heaven.

Even so while one by one lost souls are
    shriven,
A mighty multitude of quickened dead;
    Christ's love outnumbering ten times sevenfold
    seven.

Even so while man still tosses high his head,
    While still the All-Holy Spirit's strife is
    striven;—
Till one last trump shake earth, and undismayed
    Astonished Heaven.

"Judge nothing before the time."

LOVE understands the mystery, whereof
  We can but spell a surface history:
Love knows, remembers: let us trust in Love:
  Love understands the mystery.

Love weighs the event, the long pre-history,
Measures the depth beneath, the height above,
  The mystery, with the ante-mystery.

To love and to be grieved befits a dove
  Silently telling her bead-history:
Trust all to Love, be patient and approve:
  Love understands the mystery.

HOW great is little man!
  Sun, moon, and stars respond to him,
  Shine or grow dim
Harmonious with his span.

How little is great man!
  More changeable than changeful moon,
  Nor half in tune
With Heaven's harmonious plan.

Ah, rich man! ah, poor man!
  Make ready for the testing day
  When wastes away
What bears not fire or fan.

Thou heir of all things, man,
  Pursue the saints by heavenward track:
  They looked not back;
Run thou, as erst they ran.

Little and great is man:
  Great if he will, or if he will
  A pigmy still;
For what he will he can.

MAN'S life is but a working day
  Whose tasks are set aright:
A time to work, a time to pray,
  And then a quiet night.
And then, please God, a quiet night
Where palms are green and robes are white;
A long-drawn breath, a balm for sorrow,
And all things lovely on the morrow.

IF not with hope of life,
  Begin with fear of death:
Strive the tremendous life-long strife
  Breath after breath.

Bleed on beneath the rod;
  Weep on until thou see;
Turn fear and hope to love of God
  Who loveth thee.

Turn all to love, poor soul;
  Be love thy watch and ward;
Be love thy starting-point, thy goal,
  And thy reward.

"The day is at hand."

WATCH yet a while,
    Weep till that day shall dawn when thou
      shalt smile:
Watch till the day
When all save only Love shall pass away.

Then Love rejoicing shall forget to weep,
Shall hope or fear no more, or watch or sleep,
But only love and stint not, deep beyond deep.
Now we sow love in tears, but then shall reap.
Have patience as True Love's own flock of sheep.
Have patience with His Love
Who served for us, Who reigns for us above.

"Endure hardness."

A COLD wind stirs the blackthorn
    To burgeon and to blow,
Besprinkling half-green hedges
    With flakes and sprays of snow.

Thro' coldness and thro' keenness,
    Dear hearts, take comfort so:
Somewhere or other doubtless
    These make the blackthorn blow.

"Whither the Tribes go up, even the Tribes
of the Lord."

LIGHT is our sorrow for it ends to-morrow,
  Light is our death which cannot hold us fast;
So brief a sorrow can be scarcely sorrow,
  Or death be death so quickly past.

One night, no more, of pain that turns to pleasure,
  One night, no more, of weeping weeping sore;
And then the heaped-up measure beyond measure,
  In quietness for evermore.

Our face is set like flint against our trouble,
  Yet many things there are which comfort us;
This bubble is a rainbow-coloured bubble,
  This bubble-life tumultuous.

Our sails are set to cross the tossing river,
  Our face is set to reach Jerusalem;
We toil awhile, but then we rest for ever,
  Sing with all Saints and rest with them.

WHERE never tempest heaveth,
    Nor sorrow grieveth,
  Nor death bereaveth,
  Nor hope deceiveth,
      Sleep.

  Where never shame bewaileth,
  Nor serpent traileth,
  Nor death prevaileth,
  Nor harvest faileth,
      Reap.

M

MARVEL of marvels, if I myself shall behold
With mine own eyes my King in His city
of gold;
Where the least of lambs is spotless white in the
fold,
Where the least and last of saints in spotless white
is stoled,
Where the dimmest head beyond a moon is aureoled.
O saints, my beloved, now mouldering to mould
in the mould,
Shall I see you lift your heads, see your cerements
unrolled,
See with these very eyes? who now in darkness
and cold
Tremble for the midnight cry, the rapture, the tale
untold,
"The Bridegroom cometh, cometh, His Bride to
enfold."

Cold it is, my beloved, since your funeral bell was
tolled:
Cold it is, O my King, how cold alone on the
wold.

"What is that to thee? follow thou me."

LIE still, my restive heart, lie still:
God's Word to thee saith, "Wait and bear."
The good which He appoints is good,
The good which He denies were ill:
Yea, subtle comfort is thy care,
Thy hurt a help not understood.

"Friend, go up higher," to one : to one,
"Friend, enter thou My joy," He saith:
To one, "Be faithful unto death."
For some a wilderness doth flower,
Or day's work in one hour is done :—
"But thou, could'st thou not watch one hour?"

Lord, I had chosen another lot,
But then I had not chosen well;
Thy choice and only Thine is good :
No different lot, search heaven or hell,
Had blessed me fully understood ;
None other, which Thou orderest not.

"Worship God."

LORD, if Thy word had been "Worship Me
   not,
   For I than thou am holier: draw not near:"
We had besieged Thy Face with prayer and tear,
And manifold abasement in our lot,
Our crooked ground, our thorned and thistled plot;
   Envious of flawless Angels in their sphere,
   Envious of brutes, and envious of the mere
Unliving and undying unbegot.
But now Thou hast said, "Worship Me, and give
   Thy heart to Me, My child:" now therefore we
   Think twice before we stoop to worship Thee:
   We proffer half a heart while life is strong
And strung with hope; so sweet it is to live!
   Wilt Thou not wait? Yea, Thou hast waited
   long.

"Afterward he repented, and went."

LORD, when my heart was whole I kept it
    back
  And grudged to give it Thee.
Now then that it is broken, must I lack
  Thy kind word "Give it Me"?
Silence would be but just, and Thou art just.
Yet since I lie here shattered in the dust,
  With still an eye to lift to Thee,
A broken heart to give,
I think that Thou wilt bid me live,
  And answer "Give it Me."

"Are they not all Ministering Spirits?"

LORD, whomsoever Thou shalt send to me,
  Let that same be
    Mine Angel predilect:
Veiled or unveiled, benignant or austere,
Aloof or near;
    Thine, therefore mine, elect.

So may my soul nurse patience day by day,
Watch on and pray
    Obedient and at peace;
Living a lonely life in hope, in faith;
Loving till death,
    When life, not love, shall cease.

.... Lo, thou mine Angel with transfigured face
Brimful of grace,

> Brimful of love for me!
> Did I misdoubt thee all that weary while,
> Thee with a smile
>   For me as I for thee?

OUR life is long. Not so, wise Angels say
    Who watch us waste it, trembling while they
        weigh
Against eternity one squandered day.

Our life is long. Not so, the Saints protest,
Filled full of consolation and of rest:
"Short ill, long good, one long unending best."

Our life is long. Christ's word sounds different:
"Night cometh: no more work when day is
        spent."
Repent and work to-day, work and repent.

Lord, make us like Thy Host who day nor night
Rest not from adoration, their delight,
Crying "Holy, Holy, Holy," in the height.

Lord, make us like Thy Saints who wait and long
Contented: bound in hope and freed from wrong
They speed (may be) their vigil with a song.

Lord, make us like Thyself: for thirty-three
Slow years of toil seemed not too long to Thee,
That where Thou art there Thy Beloved might be.

LORD, what have I to offer? sickening fear
   And a heart-breaking loss.
Are these the cross Thou givest me? then dear
   I will account this cross.

If this is all I have, accept even this
   Poor priceless offering,
A quaking heart with all that therein is,
   O Thou my thorn-crowned King.

Accept the whole, my God, accept my heart
   And its own love within:
Wilt Thou accept us and not sift apart?
   —Only sift out my sin.

JOY is but sorrow,
   While we know
It ends to-morrow:—
   Even so!
Joy with lifted veil
Shows a face as pale
As the fair changing moon so fair and frail.

Pain is but pleasure,
   If we know
It heaps up treasure:—
   Even so!
Turn, transfigured Pain,
Sweetheart, turn again,
For fair thou art as moonrise after rain.

CAN I know it?—Nay.—
Shall I know it?—Yea,
When all mists have cleared away
For ever and aye.—

Why not then to-day?—
Who hath said thee nay?
Lift a hopeful heart and pray
In a humble way.—

Other hearts are gay.—
Ask not joy to-day:
Toil to-day along thy way
Keeping grudge at bay.—

On a past May-day
Flowers pranked all the way;
Nightingales sang out their say
On a night of May.—

Dost thou covet May
On an Autumn day?
Foolish memory saith its say
Of sweets past away.—

Gone the bloom of May,
Autumn beareth bay:
Flowerless wreath for head grown grey
Seemly were to-day.—

Dost thou covet bay?
Ask it not to-day:
Rather for a palm-branch pray;
None will say thee nay.

"When my heart is vexed I will complain."

" THE fields are white to harvest, look and see,
    Are white abundantly.
The full-orbed harvest moon shines clear,
The harvest time draws near,
Be of good cheer."

"Ah, woe is me !
I have no heart for harvest time,
Grown sick with hope deferred from chime to
    chime."

" But Christ can give thee heart Who loveth thee :
Can set thee in the eternal ecstasy
Of His great jubilee :
Can give thee dancing heart and shining face,
And lips filled full of grace,
And pleasures as the rivers and the sea.
Who knocketh at His door
He welcomes evermore :
Kneel down before
That ever-open door
(The time is short) and smite
Thy breast, and pray with all thy might."

" What shall I say ? "
                        " Nay, pray.
Tho' one but say 'Thy Will be done,'
He hath not lost his day
At set of sun."

"Praying always."

AFTER midnight, in the dark
  The clock strikes one,
    New day has begun.
Look up and hark!
With singing heart forestall the carolling lark.

After mid-day, in the light
  The clock strikes one,
    Day-fall has begun.
Cast up, set right
The day's account against the on-coming night.

After noon and night, one day
  For ever one
    Ends not, once begun.
Whither away,
O brothers and O sisters? Pause and pray.

"As thy days, so shall thy strength be."

DAY that hath no tinge of night,
  Night that hath no tinge of day,
These at last will come to sight
    Not to fade away.

This is twilight that we know,
  Scarcely night and scarcely day;
This hath been from long ago
    Shed around man's way:

Step by step to utter night,
    Step by step to perfect day,
To the Left Hand or the Right
    Leading all away.

This is twilight: be it so;
    Suited to our strength our day:
Let us follow on to know,
    Patient by the way.

A HEAVY heart, if ever heart was heavy,
    I offer Thee this heavy heart of me.
Are such as this the hearts Thou art fain to levy
    To do and dare for Thee, to bleed for Thee?
    Ah, blessed heaviness, if such they be!

Time was I bloomed with blossom and stood leafy
    How long before the fruit, if fruit there be:
Lord, if by bearing fruit my heart grows heavy,
    Leafless and bloomless yet accept of me
    The stripped fruit-bearing heart I offer Thee.

Lifted to Thee my heart weighs not so heavy.
    It leaps and lightens lifted up to Thee;
It sings, it hopes to sing amid the bevy
    Of thousand thousand choirs that sing, and see
    Thy Face, me loving, for Thou lovest me.

IF love is not worth loving, then life is not
    worth living,
Nor aught is worth remembering but well forgot;
For store is not worth storing and gifts are not
    worth giving,
    If love is not;

And idly cold is death-cold, and life-heat idly
    hot,
And vain is any offering and vainer our receiving,
And vanity of vanities is all our lot.

Better than life's heaving heart is death's heart
    unheaving,
    Better than the opening leaves are the leaves that
    rot,
For there is nothing left worth achieving or
    retrieving,
    If love is not.

WHAT is it Jesus saith unto the soul?
    "Take up the Cross, and come and
    follow Me."
One word He saith to all men: none may be
Without a cross yet hope to touch the goal.
Then heave it bravely up, and brace thy whole
    Body to bear; it will not weigh on thee
    Past strength; or if it crush thee to thy knee
Take heart of grace, for grace shall be thy dole.

Give thanks to-day, and let to-morrow take
 Heed to itself; to-day imports thee more,
  To-morrow may not dawn like yesterday:
  Until that unknown morrow go thy way,
Suffer and work and strive for Jesus' sake :—
 Who tells thee what to-morrow keeps in store?

THEY lie at rest, our blessed dead;
 The dews drop cool above their head,
They knew not when fleet summer fled.

Together all, yet each alone;
Each laid at rest beneath his own
Smooth turf or white allotted stone.

When shall our slumber sink so deep,
And eyes that wept and eyes that weep
Weep not in the sufficient sleep?

God be with you, our great and small,
Our loves, our best beloved of all,
Our own beyond the salt sea-wall.

"Ye that fear Him, both small and great."

GREAT or small below,
 Great or small above;
Be we Thine, whom Thou dost know
 And love:

First or last on earth,
　　First or last in Heaven;
Only weighted with Thy worth,
　　And shriven.

Wise or ignorant,
　　Strong or weak; Amen;
Sifted now, cast down, in want:—
　　But then?

Then,—when sun nor moon,
　　Time nor death, finds place,
Seeing in the eternal noon
　　Thy Face:

Then,—when tears and sighing,
　　Changes, sorrows, cease;
Living by Thy Life undying
　　In peace:

Then,—when all creation
　　Keeps its jubilee,
Crowned amid Thy holy nation;
Crowned, discrowned, in adoration
　　Of Thee.

"Called to be Saints."

THE lowest place.　Ah, Lord, how steep and
　　high
That lowest place whereon a saint shall sit!
Which of us halting, trembling, pressing nigh,
　　Shall quite attain to it?

Yet, Lord, Thou pressest nigh to hail and grace
  Some happy soul, it may be still unfit
For Right Hand or for Left Hand, but whose
    place
  Waits there prepared for it.

THE sinner's own fault? So it was.
  If every own fault found us out,
  Dogged us and hedged us round about,
What comfort should we take because
  Not half our due we thus wrung out?

Clearly his own fault. Yet I think
  My fault in part, who did not pray
  But lagged and would not lead the way.
I, haply, proved his missing link.
  God help us both to mend and pray.

HO cares for earthly bread tho' white?
  Nay, heavenly sheaf of harvest corn!
Who cares for earthly crown to-night?
  Nay, heavenly crown to-morrow morn!
I will not wander left or right,
  The straightest road is shortest too;
  And since we hold all hope in view
And triumph where is no more pain,
  To-night I bid good night to you
And bid you meet me there again.

LAUGHING Life cries at the feast,—
  Craving Death cries at the door,—
"Fish, or fowl, or fatted beast?"
  "Come with me, thy feast is o'er."—
"Wreathe the violets."—"Watch them fade."—
"I am sunshine."—"I am shade :
I am the sun-burying west."—
"I am pleasure."—"I am rest:
Come with me, for I am best."

"The end is not yet."

HOME by different ways. Yet all
  Homeward bound thro' prayer and praise,
Young with old, and great with small,
  Home by different ways.

  Many nights and many days
Wind must bluster, rain must fall,
  Quake the quicksand, shift the haze.

Life hath called and death will call
  Saints who praying kneel at gaze,
Ford the flood or leap the wall,
  Home by different ways.

WHO would wish back the Saints upon our rough
    Wearisome road?
      Wish back a breathless soul
      Just at the goal?
    My soul, praise God
For all dear souls which have enough.

I would not fetch one back to hope with me
    A hope deferred,
      To taste a cup that slips
      From thirsting lips :—
    Hath he not heard
And seen what was to hear and see?

How could I stand to answer the rebuke
    If one should say:
      "O friend of little faith,
      Good was my death,
    And good my day
Of rest, and good the sleep I took"?

"That which hath been is named already, and
      it is known that it is Man."

"EYE hath not seen" :—yet man hath known
    and weighed
A hundred thousand marvels that have been :
What is it which (the Word of Truth hath said)
    Eye hath not seen?

"Ear hath not heard : "—yet harpings of delight,
Trumpets of triumph, song and spoken word,
Man knows them all : what lovelier, loftier might
Hath ear not heard?

"Nor heart conceived : "—yet man hath now
desired
Beyond all reach, beyond his hope believed,
Loved beyond death : what fire shall yet be fired
No heart conceived?

"Deep calls to deep : "—man's depth would be
despair
But for God's deeper depth : we sow to reap,
Have patience, wait, betake ourselves to prayer :
Deep answereth deep.

F each sad word which is more sorrowful,
"Sorrow" or "Disappointment"? I have
heard
Subtle inflections baffling subtlest rule,
Of each sad word.

Sorrow can mourn : and lo! a mourning bird
Sings sweetly to sweet echoes of its dule,
While silent disappointment broods unstirred.

Yet both nurse hope, where Penitence keeps school
Who makes fools wise and saints of them that
erred :
Wise men shape stepping stone, or curb, or tool,
Of each sad word.

N

Songs for Strangers and Pilgrims.

"I see that all things come to an end."

I.

NO more! while sun and planets fly,
  And wind and storm and seasons four,
And while we live and while we die,—
  No more.

Nevertheless old ocean's roar,
And wide earth's multitudinous cry,
  And echo's pent reverberant store

Shall hush to silence by and bye:
  Ah, rosy world gone cold and hoar!
Man opes no more a mortal eye,
  No more.

"But Thy Commandment is exceeding broad."

II.

ONCE again to wake, nor wish to sleep;
  Once again to feel, nor feel a pain!
Rouse thy soul to watch and pray and weep
  Once again.

Hope afresh, for hope shall not be vain:
Start afresh along the exceeding steep
  Road to glory, long and rough and plain.

Sow and reap: for while these moments creep,
  Time and earth and life are on the wane:
Now, in tears; to-morrow, laugh and reap
  Once again.

Sursum Corda.

"LIFT up your hearts." "We lift them up."
        Ah me!
I cannot, Lord, lift up my heart to Thee:
Stoop, lift it up, that where Thou art I too may be.

"Give Me thy heart." I would not say Thee
        nay,
But have no power to keep or give away
My heart: stoop, Lord, and take it to Thyself
        to-day.

Stoop, Lord, as once before, now once anew
Stoop, Lord, and hearken, hearken, Lord, and do,
And take my will, and take my heart, and take
        me too.

YE, who are not dead and fit
        Like blasted tree beside the pit
But for the axe that levels it,

Living show life of love, whereof
The force wields earth and heaven above:
Who knows not love begetteth love?

Love poises earth in space, Love rolls
Wide worlds rejoicing on their poles,
And girds them round with aureoles.

Love lights the sun, Love thro' the dark
Lights the moon's evanescent arc,
Lights up the star, lights up the spark.

N 2

O ye who taste that love is sweet,
Set waymarks for all doubtful feet
That stumble on in search of it.

Sing notes of love: that some who hear
Far off inert may lend an ear,
Rise up and wonder and draw near.

Lead life of love: that others who
Behold your life, may kindle too
With love, and cast their lot with you.

WHERE shall I find a white rose blowing?—
   Out in the garden where all sweets be.—
But out in my garden the snow was snowing
   And never a white rose opened for me.
Nought but snow and a wind were blowing
     And snowing.

Where shall I find a blush rose blushing?—
   On the garden wall or the garden bed.—
But out in my garden the rain was rushing
   And never a blush rose raised its head.
Nothing glowing, flushing or blushing:
     Rain rushing.

Where shall I find a red rose budding?—
   Out in the garden where all things grow.—
But out in my garden a flood was flooding
   And never a red rose began to blow.
Out in a flooding what should be budding?
     All flooding!

Now is winter and now is sorrow,
  No roses but only thorns to-day:
Thorns will put on roses to-morrow,
  Winter and sorrow scudding away.
No more winter and no more sorrow
  To-morrow.

"Redeeming the Time."

A LIFE of hope deferred too often is
  A life of wasted opportunities;
A life of perished hope too often is
A life of all-lost opportunities:
Yet hope is but the flower and not the root,
And hope is still the flower and not the fruit;—
Arise and sow and weed: a day shall come
When also thou shalt keep thy harvest home.

"Now they desire a Better Country."

LOVE said nay, while Hope kept saying
  All his sweetest say,
Hope so keen to start a-maying!—
  Love said nay.

Love was bent to watch and pray;
Long the watching, long the praying;
  Hope grew drowsy, pale and grey.

Hope in dreams set off a-straying,
  All his dream-world flushed by May;
While unslumbering, praying, weighing,
  Love said nay.

A CASTLE-BUILDER'S WORLD.

*"The line of confusion, and the stones of
emptiness."*

UNRIPE harvest there hath none to reap it
   From the misty gusty place,
Unripe vineyard there hath none to keep it
   In unprofitable space.
Living men and women are not found there,
   Only masks in flocks and shoals ;
Flesh-and-bloodless hazy masks surround there,
   Ever wavering orbs and poles ;
Flesh-and-bloodless vapid masks abound there,
   Shades of bodies without souls.

"These all wait upon Thee."

INNOCENT eyes not ours
   Are made to look on flowers,
Eyes of small birds and insects small :
   Morn after summer morn
   The sweet rose on her thorn
Opens her bosom to them all.
   The least and last of things
   That soar on quivering wings,
Or crawl among the grass blades out of sight,
Have just as clear a right
To their appointed portion of delight
   As Queens or Kings.

"Doeth well . . . doeth better."

MY love whose heart is tender said to me,
    "A moon lacks light except her sun
        befriend her.
Let us keep tryst in heaven, dear Friend," said
    she,
My love whose heart is tender.

From such a loftiness no words could bend her:
Yet still she spoke of "us" and spoke as "we,"
    Her hope substantial, while my hope grew
        slender.

Now keeps she tryst beyond earth's utmost sea,
    Wholly at rest, tho' storms should toss and
        rend her;
And still she keeps my heart and keeps its key,
    My love whose heart is tender.

OUR heaven must be within ourselves,
    Our home and heaven the work of faith
All thro' this race of life which shelves
        Downward to death.

So faith shall build the boundary wall,
    And hope shall plant the secret bower,
That both may show magnifical
        With gem and flower.

While over all a dome must spread,
　And love shall be that dome above;
And deep foundations must be laid,
　　　　And these are love.

❖

"Vanity of Vanities."

OF all the downfalls in the world,
　The flutter of an Autumn leaf
　Grows grievous by suggesting grief:
Who thought, when Spring was first unfurled,
Of this? The wide world lay empearled;
Who thought of frost that nips the world?
　　　　　Sigh on, my ditty.

There lurk a hundred subtle stings
　To prick us in our daily walk:
　An apple cankered on its stalk,
A robin snared for all his wings,
A voice that sang but never sings;
Yea, sight or sound or silence stings.
　　　　　Kind Lord, show pity.

❖

THE hills are tipped with sunshine, while I walk
　In shadows dim and cold:
The unawakened rose sleeps on her stalk
　In a bud's fold,
　Until the sun flood all the world with gold.

The hills are crowned with glory, and the glow
  Flows widening down apace :
Unto the sunny hill-tops I, set low,
  Lift a tired face,—
  Ah, happy rose, content to wait for grace !

How tired a face, how tired a brain, how tired
  A heart I lift, who long
For something never felt but still desired ;
  Sunshine and song,
Song where the choirs of sunny heaven stand
    choired.

SCARCE tolerable life, which all life long
  Is dominated by one dread of death ;
  Is such life, life? if so, who pondereth
May call salt sweetness or call discord song.
Ah me, this solitude where swarms a throng !
  Life slowly grows and dwindles breath by breath :
  Death slowly grows on us; no word it saith,
Its cords all lengthened and its pillars strong.
Life dies apace, a life that but deceives :
  Death reigns as tho' it lived, and yet is dead :
Where is the life that dies not but that lives?
    The sweet long life, immortal, ever young,
    True life that wooes us with a silver tongue
Of hope, much said and much more left unsaid.

ALL heaven is blazing yet
  With the meridian sun:
Make haste, unshadowing sun, make haste to set;
  O lifeless life, have done.
I choose what once I chose;
  What once I willed, I will:
Only the heart its own bereavement knows;
  O clamorous heart, lie still.

That which I chose, I choose;
  That which I willed, I will;
That which I once refused, I still refuse:
  O hope deferred, be still.
That which I chose and choose
  And will is Jesus' Will:
He hath not lost his life who seems to lose:
  O hope deferred, hope still.

"Balm in Gilead."

HEARTSEASE I found, where Love-lies-bleed-
  ing
Empurpled all the ground:
Whatever flowers I missed unheeding,
Heartsease I found.

Yet still my garden mound
Stood sore in need of watering, weeding,
  And binding growths unbound.

Ah, when shades fell to light succeeding
  I scarcely dared look round:
"Love-lies-bleeding" was all my pleading,
  Heartsease I found.

"In the day of his Espousals."

THAT Song of Songs which is Solomon's
   Sinks and rises, and loves and longs,
Thro' temperate zones and torrid zones,
   That Song of Songs.

Fair its floating moon with her prongs :
Love is laid for its paving stones :
   Right it sings without thought of wrongs.

Doves it hath with music of moans,
   Queens in throngs and damsels in throngs,
High tones and mysterious undertones,
   That Song of Songs.

"She came from the uttermost part of the earth."

"THE half was not told me," said Sheba's
   Queen,
Weighing that wealth of wisdom and of gold :
" Thy fame falls short of this that I have seen :
   The half was not told.

" Happy thy servants who stand to behold,
Stand to drink in thy gracious speech and mien ;
   Happy, thrice happy, the flock of thy fold.

" As the darkened moon while a shadow between
   Her face and her kindling sun is rolled,
I depart ; but my heart keeps memory green :
   The half was not told."

ALLELUIA! or Alas! my heart is crying:
So yours is sighing;
Or replying with content undying,
Alleluia!

Alas! grieves overmuch for pain that is ending,
Hurt that is mending,
Life descending soon to be ascending,
Alleluia!

THE Passion Flower hath sprung up tall,
Hath east and west its arms outspread;
The heliotrope shoots up its head
To clear the shadow of the wall:
Down looks the Passion Flower,
The heliotrope looks upward still,
Hour by hour
On the heavenward hill.

The Passion Flower blooms red or white,
A shadowed white, a cloudless red;
Caressingly it droops its head,
Its leaves, its tendrils, from the light:
Because that lowlier flower
Looks up, but mounts not half so high,
Hour by hour
Tending toward the sky.

God's Acre.

HAIL, garden of confident hope!
  Where sweet seeds are quickening in dark-
    ness and cold;
  For how sweet and how young will they be
When they pierce thro' the mould.
Balm, myrtle, and heliotrope
  There watch and there wait out of sight for
    their Sun :
  While the Sun, which they see not, doth see
Each and all one by one.

"The Flowers appear on the Earth."

YOUNG girls wear flowers,
  Young brides a flowery wreath,
But next we plant them
  In garden plots of death.
Whose lot is best:
The maiden's curtained rest,
  Or bride's whose hoped-for sweet
  May yet outstrip her feet?
Ah! what are such as these
To death's sufficing ease?
He sleeps indeed who sleeps in peace
  Where night and morning meet.

Dear are the blossoms
    For bride's or maiden's head,
But dearer planted
    Around our blessed dead.
Those mind us of decay
And joys that fade away,
    These preach to us perfection,
    Long love and resurrection.
We make our graveyards fair,
For spirit-like birds of air,
For Angels may be finding there
    Lost Eden's own delection.

"Thou knewest . . . thou oughtest therefore."

BEHOLD in heaven a floating dazzling cloud,
  So dazzling that I could but cry Alas!
Alas, because I felt how low I was;
Alas, within my spirit if not aloud,
Foreviewing my last breathless bed and shroud:
  Thus pondering, I glanced downward on the grass;
  And the grass bowed when airs of heaven would
      pass,
Lifting itself again when it had bowed.
That grass spake comfort; weak it was and low,
  Yet strong enough and high enough to bend
    In homage at a message from the sky:
  As the grass did and prospered, so will I;
Tho' knowing little, doing what I know,
  And strong in patient weakness till the end.

"Go in Peace."

CAN peach renew lost bloom,
Or violet lost perfume,
Or sullied snow turn white as overnight?
Man cannot compass it, yet never fear:
The leper Naaman
Shows what God will and can;
God Who worked there is working here;
Wherefore let shame, not gloom, betinge thy brow,
God Who worked then is working now.

"Half Dead."

O CHRIST the Life, look on me where I lie
Ready to die:
O Good Samaritan, nay, pass not by.

O Christ, my Life, pour in Thine oil and wine
To keep me Thine;
Me ever Thine, and Thee for ever mine.

Watch by Thy saints and sinners, watch by all
Thy great and small:
Once Thou didst call us all,—O Lord, recall.

Think how Thy saints love sinners, how they pray
And hope alway,
And thereby grow more like Thee day by day.

O Saint of saints, if those with prayer and vow
Succour us now. . . .
It was not they died for us, it was Thou.

"One of the Soldiers with a Spear pierced His Side."

AH, Lord, we all have pierced Thee: wilt
Thou be
Wroth with us all to slay us all?
Nay, Lord, be this thing far from Thee and me:
By whom should we arise, for we are small,
By whom if not by Thee?

Lord, if of us who pierced Thee Thou spare one,
Spare yet one more to love Thy Face,
And yet another of poor souls undone,
Another, and another—God of grace,
Let mercy overrun.

❖

WHERE love is, there comes sorrow
To-day or else to-morrow:
Endure the mood,
Love only means our good.

Where love is, there comes pleasure
With or withouten measure,
Early or late
Cheering the sorriest state.

Where love is, all perfection
Is stored for heart's delection;
For where love is
Dwells every sort of bliss.

Who would not choose a sorrow
Love's self will cheer to-morrow?
One day of sorrow,
Then such a long to-morrow!

BURY Hope out of sight,
  No book for it and no bell;
It never could bear the light
  Even while growing and well:
Think if now it could bear
The light on its face of care
And grey scattered hair.

No grave for Hope in the earth,
  But deep in that silent soul
Which rang no bell for its birth
  And rings no funeral toll.
Cover its once bright head;
Nor odours nor tears be shed:
It lived once, it is dead.

Brief was the day of its power,
  The day of its grace how brief:
As the fading of a flower,
  As the falling of a leaf,   ·
So brief its day and its hour;
No bud more and no bower
Or hint of a flower.

Shall many wail it? not so:
  Shall one bewail it? not one:
Thus it hath been from long ago,
  Thus it shall be beneath the sun.
O fleet sun, make haste to flee;
O rivers, fill up the sea;
O Death, set the dying free.

The sun nor loiters nor speeds,
  The rivers run as they ran.
Thro' clouds or thro' windy reeds
  All run as when all began.
Only Death turns at our cries:—
Lo, the Hope we buried with sighs
Alive in Death's eyes!

A Churchyard Song of Patient Hope.

ALL tears done away with the bitter unquiet
    sea,
Death done away from among the living at last,
Man shall say of sorrow—Love grant it to thee and
    me!—
  At last, "It is past."

Shall I say of pain, "It is past," nor say it with
    thee,
  Thou heart of my heart, thou soul of my soul,
    my Friend?
Shalt thou say of pain, "It is past," nor say it
    with me
  Beloved to the end?

ONE woe is past. Come what come will
  Thus much is ended and made fast:
Two woes may overhang us still;
  One woe is past.

As flowers when winter puffs its last
Wake in the vale, trail up the hill,
  Nor wait for skies to overcast;

So meek souls rally from the chill
  Of pain and fear and poisonous blast,
To lift their heads: come good, come ill,
  One woe is past.

"Take no thought for the morrow."

WHO knows? God knows: and what He
    knows
  Is well and best.
The darkness hideth not from Him, but glows
Clear as the morning or the evening rose
  Of east or west.

Wherefore man's strength is to sit still:
  Not wasting care
To antedate to-morrow's good or ill;
Yet watching meekly, watching with good will,
  Watching to prayer.

Some rising or some setting ray
  From east or west,
If not to-day, why then another day
Will light each dove upon the homeward way
  Safe to her nest.

"Consider the Lilies of the field."

SOLOMON most glorious in array
 Put not on his glories without care :—
Clothe us as Thy lilies of a day,
 As the lilies Thou accountest fair,
  Lilies of Thy making,
  Of Thy love partaking,
 Filling with free fragrance earth and air :
 Thou Who gatherest lilies, gather us and wear

"Son, remember."

LAID beside thy gate, am Lazarus ;
 See me or see me not I still am there,
 Hungry and thirsty, sore and sick and bare,
Dog-comforted and crumbs-solicitous :
While thou in all thy ways art sumptuous,
 Daintily clothed, with dainties for thy fare :
 Thus a world's wonder thou art quit of care,
And be I seen or not seen I am thus.
One day a worm for thee, a worm for me :
 With my worm angel songs and trumpet burst
  And plenitude an end of all desire :
But what for thee, alas ! but what for thee ?
 Fire and an unextinguishable thirst,
  Thirst in an unextinguishable fire.

"Heaviness may endure for a night, but Joy
cometh in the morning."

NO thing is great on this side of the grave,
  Nor any thing of any stable worth:
Whatso is born from earth returns to earth:
No thing we grasp proves half the thing we
    crave:
The tidal wave shrinks to the ebbing wave:
  Laughter is folly, madness lurks in mirth:
  Mankind sets off a-dying from the birth:
Life is a losing game, with what to save?
Thus I sat mourning like a mournful owl,
  And like a doleful dragon made ado,
    Companion of all monsters of the dark:
When lo! the light cast off its nightly cowl,
    And up to heaven flashed a carolling lark,
  And all creation sang its hymn anew.

While all creation sang its hymn anew
  What could I do but sing a stave in tune?
  Spectral on high hung pale the vanishing
    moon
Where a last gleam of stars hung paling too.
Lark's lay—a cockcrow—with a scattered few
  Soft early chirpings—with a tender croon
  Of doves—a hundred thousand calls, and soon
A hundred thousand answers sweet and true.
These set me singing too at unawares:
  One note for all delights and charities,
    One note for hope reviving with the light,
  One note for every lovely thing that is;
Till while I sang my heart shook off its cares
    And revelled in the land of no more night.

"The Will of the Lord be done."

LORD, fulfil Thy Will
    Be the days few or many, good or ill:
Prolong them, to suffice
For offering up ourselves Thy sacrifice;
Shorten them if Thou wilt,
To make in righteousness an end of guilt.
Yea, they will not be long
To souls who learn to sing a patient song;
Yea, short they will not be
To souls on tiptoe to flee home to Thee.
O Lord, fulfil Thy Will:
Make Thy Will ours, and keep us patient still
Be the days few or many, good or ill.

"Lay up for yourselves treasures in Heaven."

TREASURE plies a feather,
    Pleasure spreadeth wings,
Taking flight together,—
    Ah! my cherished things.

Fly away, poor pleasure,
    That art so brief a thing:
Fly away, poor treasure,
    That hast so swift a wing.

Pleasure, to be pleasure,
    Must come without a wing:
Treasure, to be treasure,
    Must be a stable thing.

Treasure without feather,
Pleasure without wings,
Elsewhere dwell together
And are heavenly things.

"Whom the Lord loveth he chasteneth."

" ONE sorrow more? I thought the tale
complete."—
He bore amiss who grudges what he bore:
Stretch out thy hands and urge thy feet to meet
One sorrow more.

Yea, make thy count for two or three or
four :
The kind Physician will not slack to treat
His patient while there's rankling in the sore.

Bear up in anguish, ease will yet be sweet;
Bear up all day, for night has rest in store :
Christ bears thy burden with thee, rise and greet
One sorrow more.

"Then shall ye shout."

IT seems an easy thing
Mayhap one day to sing;
Yet the next day
We cannot sing or say.

Keep silence with good heart,
While silence fits our part:
Another day
We shall both sing and say.

Keep silence, counting time
To strike in at the chime:
Prepare to sound,—
Our part is coming round.

Can we not sing or say?
In silence let us pray,
And meditate
Our love-song while we wait.

EVERYTHING that is born must die;
  Everything that can sigh may sing;
Rocks in equal balance, low or high,
  Everything.

Honeycomb is weighed against a sting;
Hope and fear take turns to touch the sky;
  Height and depth respond alternating.

O my soul, spread wings of love to fly,
  Wings of dove that soars on home-bound wing:
Love trusts Love, till Love shall justify
  Everything.

LORD, grant us calm, if calm can set forth
  Thee;
 Or tempest, if a tempest set Thee forth;
 Wind from the east or west or south or north,
Or congelation of a silent sea,
With stillness of each tremulous aspen tree.

Still let fruit fall, or hang upon the tree;
 Still let the east and west, the south and north,
Curb in their winds, or plough a thundering sea;
 Still let the earth abide to set Thee forth,
Or vanish like a smoke to set forth Thee.

Changing Chimes.

IT was not warning that our fathers lacked,
 It is not warning that we lack to-day.
The Voice that cried still cries: "Rise up and act:
 Watch alway,—watch and pray,—watch alway,—
       All men."

Alas, if aught was lacked goodwill was lacked;
 Alas, goodwill is what we lack to-day.
O gracious Voice, grant grace that all may act,
 Watch and act, — watch and pray, — watch
  alway.—   Amen.

"Thy Servant will go and fight with this Philistine."

SORROW of saints is sorrow of a day,
  Gladness of saints is gladness evermore:
Send on thy hope, send on thy will before
To chant God's praise along the narrow way.
Stir up His praises if the flesh would sway,
  Exalt His praises if the world press sore,
  Peal out His praises if black Satan roar
A hundred thousand lies to say them nay.
Devil and Death and Hades, threefold cord
Not quickly broken, front thee to thy face;
    Front thou them with a face of tenfold flint:
    Shout for the battle, David! never stint
Body or breath or blood, but proof in grace
Die for thy Lord, as once for thee thy Lord.

THRO' burden and heat of the day
  How weary the hands and the feet
That labour with scarcely a stay,
  Thro' burden and heat!

Tired toiler whose sleep shall be sweet,
Kneel down, it will rest thee to pray:
  Then forward, for daylight is fleet.

Cool shadows show lengthening and grey,
  Cool twilight will soon be complete:
What matters this wearisome way
  Thro' burden and heat?

"Then I commended Mirth."

"A MERRY heart is a continual feast."
  Then take we life and all things in good
    part:
To fast grows festive while we keep at least
  A merry heart

Well pleased with nature and well pleased with
    art;
A merry heart makes cheer for man and beast,
And fancies music in a creaking cart.

Some day, a restful heart whose toils have ceased,
  A heavenly heart gone home from earthly mart:
To-day, blow wind from west or wind from east,
  A merry heart.

SORROW hath a double voice,
  Sharp to-day but sweet to-morrow:
Wait in patience, hope, rejoice,
  Tried friends of sorrow.

Pleasure hath a double taste,
  Sweet to-day but sharp to-morrow:
Friends of pleasure, rise in haste,
  Make friends with sorrow.

Pleasure set aside to-day
  Comes again to rule to-morrow:
Welcomed sorrow will not stay,
  Farewell to sorrow!

SHADOWS to-day, while shadows show God's
    Will.
  Light were not good except He sent us light.
  Shadows to-day, because this day is night
Whose marvels and whose mysteries fulfil
Their course and deep in darkness serve Him still.
  Thou dim aurora, on the extremest height
  Of airy summits wax not over-bright;
Refrain thy rose, refrain thy daffodil.
Until God's Word go forth to kindle thee
    And garland thee and bid thee stoop to us,
      Blush in the heavenly choirs and glance not
        down:
    To-day we race in darkness for a crown,
In darkness for beatitude to be,
    In darkness for the city luminous.

"Truly the Light is sweet."

LIGHT colourless doth colour all things else:
    Where light dwells pleasure dwells
And peace excels.
    Then rise and shine,
    Thou shadowed soul of mine,
    And let a cheerful rainbow make thee fine.

Light, fountain of all beauty and delight,
Leads day forth from the night,
Turns blackness white.
    Light waits for thee
    Where all have eyes to see:
    Oh, well is thee, and happy shalt thou be!

"Are ye not much better than they?"

THE twig sprouteth,
The moth outeth,
The plant springeth,
The bird singeth:
Tho' little we sing to-day
Yet are we better than they;
Tho' growing with scarce a showing,
Yet, please God, we are growing.

The twig teacheth,
The moth preacheth,
The plant vaunteth,
The bird chanteth,
God's mercy overflowing
Merciful past man's knowing.
Please God to keep us growing
Till the awful day of mowing.

"Yea, the sparrow hath found her an house."

WISEST of sparrows that sparrow which sitteth
alone
Perched on the housetop, its own upper chamber,
for nest;
Wisest of swallows that swallow which timely has
flown
Over the turbulent sea to the land of its rest:
Wisest of sparrows and swallows, if I were
as wise!

Wisest of spirits that spirit which dwelleth apart
  Hid in the Presence of God for a chapel and
    nest,
Sending a wish and a will and a passionate heart
  Over the eddy of life to that Presence in rest:
    Seated alone and in peace till God bids it
    arise.

"I am small and of no reputation."

THE least, if so I am;
  If so, less than the least,
May I reach heaven to glorify the Lamb
  And sit down at the Feast.

I fear and I am small,
  Whence am I of good cheer;
For I who hear Thy call, have heard Thee call
  To Thee the small who fear.

O CHRIST my God Who seest the unseen,
  O Christ my God Who knowest the un-
    known,
  Thy mighty Blood was poured forth to atone
For every sin that can be or hath been.

O Thou Who seest what I cannot see,
  Thou Who didst love us all so long ago,
  O Thou Who knowest what I must not know,
Remember all my hope, remember me.

YEA, if Thou wilt, Thou canst put up Thy
    sword;
But what if Thou shouldst sheathe it to the hilt
Within the heart that sues to Thee, O Lord?
    Yea, if Thou wilt.

For if Thou wilt Thou canst purge out the guilt
Of all, of any, even the most abhorred:
    Thou canst pluck down, rebuild, build up the
      unbuilt.

Who wanders, canst Thou gather by love's cord?
    Who sinks, uplift from the under-sucking silt
To set him on Thy rock within Thy ward?
    Yea, if Thou wilt.

SWEETNESS of rest when Thou sheddest rest,
    Sweetness of patience till then;
Only the Will of our God is best
    For all the millions of men.

For all the millions on earth to-day,
    On earth and under the earth;
Waiting for earth to vanish away,
    Waiting to come to the birth.

FOOLISH Soul! to make thy count
    For languid falls and much forgiven,
When like a flame thou mightest mount
    To storm and carry heaven.

A life so faint,—is this to live?
  A goal so mean,—is this a goal?
Christ love thee, remedy, forgive,
    Save thee, O foolish Soul.

BEFORE the beginning Thou hast foreknown
  the end,
  Before the birthday the death-bed was seen of
    Thee:
Cleanse what I cannot cleanse, mend what I cannot
  mend,
  O Lord All-Merciful, be merciful to me.

While the end is drawing near I know not mine
  end;
  Birth I recall not, my death I cannot foresee:
O God, arise to defend, arise to befriend,
  O Lord All-Merciful, be merciful to me.

THE goal in sight! Look up and sing,
  Set faces full against the light,
Welcome with rapturous welcoming
  The goal in sight.

Let be the left, let be the right:
Straight forward make your footsteps ring
  A loud alarum thro' the night.

Death hunts you, yea, but reft of sting;
  Your bed is green, your shroud is white:
Hail! Life and Death and all that bring
  The goal in sight.

Songs for Strangers and Pilgrims.

LOOKING back along life's trodden way
    Gleams and greenness linger on the track;
Distance melts and mellows all to-day,
      Looking back.

Rose and purple and a silvery grey,
    Is that cloud the cloud we called so black?
Evening harmonizes all to-day,
      Looking back.

Foolish feet so prone to halt or stray,
    Foolish heart so restive on the rack!
Yesterday we sighed, but not to-day
      Looking back.

✢

INDEX OF FIRST LINES.

	PAGE
A baby is a harmless thing	55
A burdened heart that bleeds and bears . . .	113
A chill blank world. Yet over the utmost sea .	46
A cold wind stirs the blackthorn	176
After midnight, in the dark	185
A heavy heart, if ever heart was heavy . .	186
Ah, Lord, Lord, if my heart were right with Thine	13
Ah, Lord, we all have pierced Thee: wilt Thou be	208
Ah me, that I should be	22
Alas, alas! for the self-destroyed	125
A life of hope deferred too often is . . .	197
All beneath the sun hasteth	107
Alleluia! or Alas! my heart is crying . .	204
All heaven is blazing yet	202
All tears done away with the bitter unquiet sea .	210
All that we see rejoices in the sunshine . .	109
All things are fair, if we had eyes to see . .	131
All weareth, all wasteth	86
Alone Lord God, in Whom our trust and peace .	7
A lovely city in a lovely land	155
"A merry heart is a continual feast" . .	219
A moon impoverished amid stars curtailed . .	106
A rose, a lily, and the Face of Christ . . .	35
"As dying, and behold we live!" . . .	165
As flames that consume the mountains, as winds that coerce the sea	159

P 2

PAGE

As froth on the face of the deep   125
As grains of sand, as stars, as drops of dew.   .   .   95
"As many as I love."—Ah, Lord, Who lovest all   .   80
As one red rose in a garden where all other roses are white   36
As the dove which found no rest   .   .   .   35
As the voice of many waters all saints sing as one   .   161
Astonished Heaven looked on when man was made   .   173
As violets so be I recluse and sweet   .   .   .   114
At sound as of rushing wind, and sight as of fire   .   80

Because Thy Love hath sought me   .   .   .   43
Be faithful unto death.   Christ proffers thee   .   115
Before the beginning Thou hast foreknown the end   .   224
Behold in heaven a floating dazzling cloud .   .   206
Behold, the Bridegroom cometh : go ye out   .   51
"Beloved, let us love one another," says St. John   57
Beloved, yield thy time to God, for He   .   .   138
Bone to his bone, grain to his grain of dust   .   168
Bring me to see, Lord, bring me yet to see .   .   164
Bury Hope out of sight   .   .   .   209
By Thy long-drawn anguish to atone .   .   .   70

Can I know it ?—Nay   183
Can man rejoice who lives in hourly fear   .   108
Can peach renew lost bloom   .   .   207
Cast down but not destroyed, chastened not slain   157
Christmas hath a darkness .   .   .   54
Christ's Heart was wrung for me, if mine is sore .   37
Clother of the lily, Feeder of the sparrow   .   38
Contempt and pangs and haunting fears   .   20
Content to come, content to go .   .   .   115
Crimson as the rubies, crimson as the roses .   .   159

Darkness and light are both alike to Thee .   .   38
Day and night the Accuser makes no pause.   .   41
Day that hath no tinge of night .   .   .   185
Dear Angels and dear disembodied Saints .   .   168

Earth cannot bar flame from ascending   .   .   56
Earth grown old, yet still so green   .   .   .   52

Index of First Lines.

	PAGE
Earth has clear call of daily bells	129
Everything that is born must die	216
Experience bows a sweet contented face	105
"Eye hath not seen":—yet man hath known and weighed	192
Fear, Faith, and Hope have sent their hearts above	116
Foul is she and ill-favoured, set askew	123
Friends, I commend to you the narrow way	37
Golden haired, lily white	156
Good Lord, to-day	65
Grant us, O Lord, that patience and that faith	117
Grant us such grace that we may work Thy Will	114
Great or small below	188
Hail, garden of confident hope	205
Hark! the Alleluias of the great salvation	97
Have dead men long to wait	169
Have I not striven, my God, and watched and prayed	40
Heartsease I found, where Love-lies-bleeding	202
Heaven is not far, tho' far the sky	130
Heaven's chimes are slow, but sure to strike at last	143
He bore an agony whereof the name	94
Herself a rose, who bore the Rose	87
Hidden from the darkness of our mortal sight	155
Home by different ways. Yet all	191
Hope is the counterpoise of fear	104
How can one man, how can all men	164
How great is little man	174
How know I that it looms lovely that land I have never seen	45
If I should say "my heart is in my home"	25
If love is not worth loving, then life is not worth living	187
If not with hope of life	175
I followed Thee, my God, I followed Thee	90
If thou be dead, forgive and thou shalt live	107
I laid beside thy gate, am Lazarus	212
I lift mine eyes, and see	68
I lift mine eyes to see : earth vanisheth	130
I long for joy, O Lord, I long for gold	13

	PAGE
I, Lord, Thy foolish sinner low and small	32
Innocent eyes not ours	198
In tempest and storm blackness of darkness for ever	126
In that world we weary to attain	138
In weariness and painfulness St. Paul	83
I peered within, and saw a world of sin	129
Is any grieved or tired? Yea, by God's Will	66
I saw a Saint.—How canst thou tell that he	66
Is this that Name as ointment poured forth	28
Is this the end? is there no end but this	124
I think of the saints I have known, and lift up mine eyes	165
It is good to be last not first	65
It is not death, O Christ, to die for Thee	10
It is the greatness of Thy Love, dear Lord, that we would celebrate	67
It seems an easy thing	215
It was not warning that our fathers lacked	217
I was hungry, and Thou feddest me	33
Jerusalem is built of gold	151
Jerusalem of fire	152
Jesus, Lord God from all eternity	23
Joy is but sorrow	182
Laughing Life cries at the feast	191
"Launch out into the deep," Christ spake of old	89
Leaf from leaf Christ knows	25
Lie still, my restive heart, lie still	178
Life that was born to-day	103
Lift up thine eyes to seek the invisible	158
"Lift up your hearts." "We lift them up." Ah me	195
Light colourless doth colour all things else	220
Light is our sorrow for it ends to-morrow	177
Little Lamb, who lost thee	29
Long and dark the nights, dim and short the days	84
Looking back along life's trodden way	225
Lord Babe, if Thou art He	59
Lord, by what inconceivable dim road	156
Lord, carry me.—Nay, but I grant thee strength	26
Lord, dost Thou look on me, and will not I	42
Lord, give me blessed fear	104

Index of First Lines.

	PAGE
Lord, give me grace	116
Lord, give me love that I may love Thee much .	101
Lord God of Hosts most Holy and most High .	23
Lord, grant me grace to love Thee in my pain .	14
Lord, grant us calm, if calm can set forth Thee .	217
Lord, grant us eyes to see and ears to hear .	11
Lord, grant us grace to mount by steps of grace .	39
Lord, grant us grace to rest upon Thy word .	117
Lord, grant us wills to trust Thee with such aim .	9
Lord, hast Thou so loved us, and will not we .	34
Lord, I am feeble and of mean account .	111
Lord, I am here.—But, child, I look for thee .	27
Lord, I believe, help Thou mine unbelief . .	11
Lord, if Thy word had been " Worship Me not" .	179
Lord Jesus Christ, grown faint upon the Cross .	73
Lord Jesus Christ, our Wisdom and our Rest .	82
Lord Jesus, who would think that I am Thine .	23
Lord Jesu, Thou art sweetness to my soul . .	32
Lord, make me one with Thine own faithful ones.	15
Lord, make me pure	110
Lord, make us all love all : that when we meet .	9
Lord, purge our eyes to see	46
Lord, to Thine own grant watchful hearts and eyes	93
Lord, we are rivers running to thy sea . . .	20
Lord, what have I that I may offer Thee . .	24
Lord, what have I to offer? sickening fear . .	182
Lord, when my heart was whole I kept it back .	180
Lord, whomsoever Thou shalt send to me . .	180
Love came down at Christmas . . .	56
Love doth so grace and dignify . . .	102
Love is alone the worthy law of love . . .	63
Love is the key of life and death . . .	98
Love loveth Thee, and wisdom loveth Thee .	101
Love said nay, while Hope kept saying . .	197
Love still is Love. and doeth all things well .	30
Love, to be love, must walk Thy way . . .	110
Love understands the mystery, whereof . .	174
Lying a-dying	167
Man's harvest is past, his summer is ended . .	147
Man's life is but a working day . . .	175

Index of First Lines.

	PAGE
Man's life is death. Yet Christ endured to live . .	70
Marvel of marvels, if I myself shall behold . . .	178
Me and my gift: kind Lord, behold . . .	30
My God, my God, have mercy on my sin . . .	64
My God, Thyself being Love Thy heart is love . .	82
My God, wilt Thou accept, and will not we . .	46
My harvest is done, its promise is ended . . .	146
My heart is yearning	44
My love whose heart is tender said to me . . .	199
Nerve us with patience, Lord, to toil or rest . .	8
New creatures ; the Creator still the Same . . .	27
No Cherub's heart or hand for us might ache . .	73
No more ! while sun and planets fly . . .	194
None other Lamb, none other Name . . .	36
No thing is great on this side of the grave . . .	213
O blessed Paul elect to grace	83
O Christ my God Who seest the unseen . . .	222
O Christ our All in each, our All in all . .	43
O Christ our Light Whom even in darkness we . .	15
O Christ the Life, look on me where I lie . .	207
Of all the downfalls in the world . . .	200
Of each sad word which is more sorrowful . .	193
O Firstfruits of our grain	84
O foolish soul ! to make thy count . . .	223
Oh fallen star ! a darkened light . . .	124
Oh knell of a passing time	140
Oh what is earth, that we should build . .	137
O Jesu, better than Thy gifts . . .	47
O Jesu, gone so far apart	89
O Lord Almighty, Who hast formed us weak . .	78
O Lord, fulfil Thy Will	214
O Lord God, hear the silence of each soul . .	12
O Lord, I am ashamed to seek Thy Face . .	10
O Lord, on Whom we gaze and dare not gaze . .	12
O Lord, seek us, O Lord, find us . . .	121
O Lord, when Thou didst call me, didst Thou know .	21
O mine enemy	41
Once again to wake, nor wish to sleep . . .	194

	PAGE
Once I ached for thy dear sake	69
Once like a broken bow Mark sprang aside	88
Once slain for Him Who first was slain for them	96
Once within, within for evermore	161
"One sorrow more? I thought the tale complete"	215
One step more, and the race is ended	61
One woe is past. Come what come will	210
O Shepherd with the bleeding Feet	29
Our heaven must be within ourselves	199
Our life is long. Not so, wise Angels say	181
Our Mothers, lovely women pitiful	166
Out in the rain a world is growing green	76
O ye, who are not dead and fit	195
O ye who love to-day	102
Parting after parting	144
Patience must dwell with Love, for Love and Sorrow	108
Piteous my rhyme is	64
Purity born of a Maid	85
Rest remains when all is done	144
Roses on a brier	134
Safe where I cannot lie yet	167
St. Barnabas, with John his sister's son	88
St. Peter once: "Lord, dost Thou wash my feet?"	90
Saints are like roses when they flush rarest	97
Scarce tolerable life, which all life long	201
Service and strength, God's Angels and Archangels	94
Seven vials hold Thy wrath: but what can hold	8
Shadows to-day, while shadows show God's Will	220
Shall not the Judge of all the earth do right	30
Short is time, and only time is bleak	146
Slain for man, slain for me, O Lamb of God, look down	31
Slain in their high places: fallen on rest	160
So brief a life, and then an endless life	142
Solomon most glorious in array	212
Sooner or later: yet at last	52
Sorrow hath a double voice	219
Sorrow of saints is sorrow of a day	218

Index of First Lines.

	PAGE
Such is Love, it comforts in extremity . . .	106
Sweetness of rest when Thou sheddest rest . .	223
Tempest and terror below; but Christ the Almighty above	40
That Eden of earth's sunrise cannot vie . .	62
That Song of Songs which is Solomon's . .	203
The end of all things is at hand. We all .	98
"The fields are white to harvest, look and see" .	184
The goal in sight! Look up and sing . .	224
The great Vine left its glory to reign as Forest King .	71
The half moon shows a face of plaintive sweetness	139
"The half was not told me," said Sheba's Queen .	203
The hills are tipped with sunshine, while I walk .	200
The joy of Saints, like incense turned to fire .	163
The King's Daughter is all glorious within . .	153
The least, if so I am	223
The lowest place. Ah, Lord, how steep and high	189
The night is far spent, the day is at hand . .	135
The Passion Flower hath sprung up tall . .	204
The sea laments with unappeasable . . .	133
The shout of a King is among them. One day may I be	160
The sinner's own fault? So it was . .	190
The tempest over and gone, the calm begun .	74
The twig sprouteth	221
The world,—what a world, ah me . .	121
They lie at rest, our blessed dead . .	188
They scarcely waked before they slept . .	57
They throng from the east and the west . .	140
This near-at-hand land breeds pain by measure .	132
Thro' burden and heat of the day . .	218
Thy Cross cruciferous doth flower in all . .	74
Thy fainting spouse, yet still Thy spouse . .	44
Thy lilies drink the dew	112
Thy lovely saints do bring Thee love . .	19
Thy Name, O Christ, as incense streaming forth .	28
Time lengthening, in the lengthening seemeth long .	142
Time passeth away with its pleasure and pain .	141
Time seems not short	139

	PAGE
Together once, but never more	145
"Together with my dead body shall they arise" .	77
Toll, bell, toll. For hope is flying . . .	126
Treasure plies a feather	214
Tremble, thou earth, at the Presence of the Lord .	141
Trembling before Thee we fall down to adore Thee .	60
Tumult and turmoil, trouble and toil . . .	42
Tune me, O Lord, into one harmony . . .	111
Unripe harvest there hath none to reap it . .	198
Unspotted lambs to follow the one Lamb . .	58
Up, my drowsing eyes	95
Up Thy Hill of Sorrows	72
Voices from above and from beneath . . .	134
Watch yet a while	176
We are of those who tremble at Thy word . .	135
Weigh all my faults and follies righteously . .	14
We know not a voice of that River . . .	81
We know not when, we know not where . .	136
What are these lovely ones, yea, what are these .	163
What is it Jesus saith unto the soul . . .	187
What is the beginning? Love. What the course?	
Love still	109
What is this above thy head	122
When all the overwork of life . . .	131
When Christ went up to Heaven the Apostles stayed .	79
When sick of life and all the world . .	136
When wickedness is broken as a tree . . .	152
Where love is, there comes sorrow . . .	208
Where never tempest heaveth	177
Where shall I find a white rose blowing . .	196
Whereto shall we liken this Blessed Mary Virgin .	86
While Christ lay dead the widowed world . .	75
Whiteness most white. Ah, to be clean again .	112
Who cares for earthly bread tho' white . .	190
Who is this that cometh up not alone . .	154
Who knows? God knows: and what He knows .	211
Who scatters tares shall reap no wheat . .	78

Index of First Lines.

	PAGE
Who sits with the King in His Throne? Not a slave but a Bride	154
Whoso hath anguish is not dead in sin . . .	105
Who would wish back the Saints upon our rough .	192
Wisest of sparrows that sparrow which sitteth alone .	221
Words cannot utter	75
Yea, blessed and holy is he that hath part in the First Resurrection	162
Yea, if Thou wilt, Thou canst put up Thy sword .	223
Yet earth was very good in days of old . . .	61
Young girls wear flowers	205